They'll Never Catch You Now

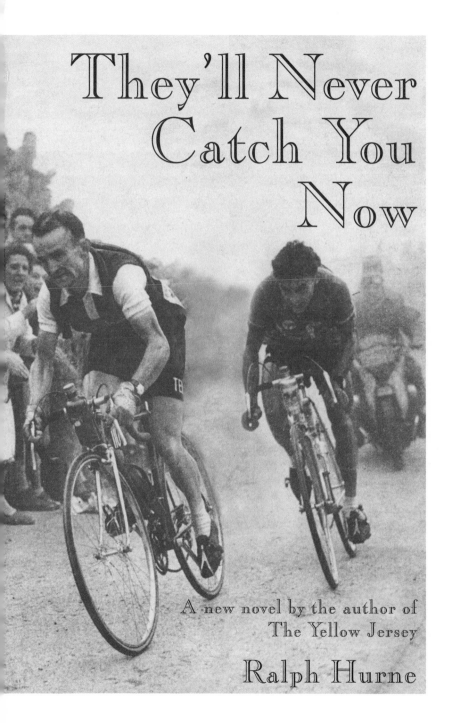

They'll Never Catch You Now

A new novel by the author of
The Yellow Jersey

Ralph Hurne

Copyright © Ralph Hurne, 2007

Printed in USA

Published by:
Van der Plas Publications / Cycle Publishing
1282 7th Avenue
San Francisco, CA 94122, U.S.A.
Tel: (415) 665-8214
Fax: (415) 753-8572
E-mail: con.tact@cyclepublishing.com
Web site: http://www.cyclepublishing.com

Distributed to the book trade by:
USA: Midpoint Trade Books, Kansas City, KS
Great Britain: Orca Book Services / Chris Lloyd Sales and Marketing
                     Services, Poole, Dorset
Australia: Tower Books, Frenchs Forest, NSW

Cover design: Rob van der Plas

Frontispiece: Robic and Le Guilly, ahead of the pack, battle it out
                     in the fog on the Tourmalet in the 1953 Tour de France

Publisher's Cataloging in Publication Data
Hurne, 1936—
They'll Never Catch You Now: A new novel by the author of
The Yellow Jersey
p. 21.6 cm
1. Bicycle Racing; 2, Novels
I. Authorship; II. Title
ISBN 978-1-892495-56-3
Library of Congress Control Number 2007921649

Contents

1. No Sad Songs 9

2. My Indecision is Final 17

3. Life in the Old Dogs 26

4. Don't Cry for Me 31

5. Funny Old World 37

6. Middlemen 49

7. Shame About the Limp 60

8. Of All the Gin Joints in All the Towns... 67

9. Catch a Falling Star 80

10. La Vie en Rose 86

11. Best Laid Plans 92

12. Vélos Mickey Mouse, Moscow 99

13. The Way We Were 107

14. Rosehip Tea 115

15. They'll Never Take Me Alive 125

16. Pennies From Heaven 139

17. May the Gods Preserve 147

18. I Shall Return 153

19. The Hammer Comes Down 164

20. Today a Rooster, Tomorrow a Feather Duster . . 180

21. You Dropped the Tour 185

    About the Author *200*

1. No Sad Songs

"Whichever way you look at it, you're over the hill." Fred Ryan straightened up and stuck a thumb in his belt.

For a second I stared at his belly over-hang.

"Over the hill," he repeated in a quieter tone, searching my face for any effect his words were having.

I leaned back in his comfortable office chair and looked at him. Behind his glasses, his eyes shone like freshly minted coins.

Quieter still he went on, "Look, Terry, it comes to us all. Look at me! Once 'round the block and I'd need artificial respiration. Let's face it, you've had a good run. Do us one more little favor and call it a day."

"Oh, I know, I know." Even to me, my voice sounded like someone else's. "And you want me to ride a stage or two in next year's Tour de France simply because of this year's near win. It was a fluke, Fred, a fluke, but you think I'll attract a fair bit of publicity for our advertisers."

He sat down heavily and spun half a turn in his swivel chair. "Well, put like that, yes. But it's their involvement that makes the whole business of pro cycling possible. We owe it to them, really, don't we? I'm not asking you to seriously contemplate another full Tour de France. Not after it nearly killed you last time. Good grief—when I saw you go down, I thought for a moment you'd had it.

"No, no, just do a stage or two. The cameras will be on you giving our sponsor's name plenty of prominence. Then just quit, pull out. And while you're in the race, you can give Romain your support like you did before. God alone knows he needs it. I know it's hard to face up to old father time and look him squarely in the face."

Ryan was full of homilies and clichés. He assured me once that he was well-read, but I've never seen or heard any evidence. The trouble was, he didn't know the shit I was in.

"Okay, okay," I found myself saying, although I had no way of knowing if I'd be around to keep my word. But giving him the nod would at least have kept him quiet.

"You don't look sure," he said sharply.

I found I hadn't got enough steam to tell him my troubles. "Oh, it's the thought of all that training, just when I'd imagined I'd waved it all goodbye."

"Fair enough," he said, but I knew he wasn't sure of me and could smell my dilemma.

Outside, in my car, I sat wondering if I should go back and tell him I'd changed my mind. Even square with the guy and tell him my whole world had collapsed. Tell him my comfortable future had disappeared in a flash. Tell him my future with the wealthy Paula had been snuffed out when she caught me providing a quick service with her daughter Susan. It wasn't much to get steamed up about. I shall pass this way but once. What have I done? I'd been asking myself for weeks. Sure, sure, I'd been a silly sod. Even worse, Susan is sort of Romain's girlfriend, and it's Romain who's looked upon as my protégé and team mate. Susan had handed it to me on a plate, otherwise I wouldn't have done the deed, even though that deed was spread over several sittings.

My accumulated wealth wasn't much, certainly not enough to see me comfortably out. Before Paula, there had been this Michelle, who was also well-heeled, and at odd moments even now I find my thoughts drifting back to her. But with my luck, would she have me? I have a mental snapshot of myself silhouetted against a rising full moon, tip-toeing away with a suitcase in each hand. That was the last I saw of her.

I decided to run through it all with my mate Throbbo, the only person I could fully confide in. Having a friend as a team mate in the ups and downs, carve-ups, and shaky loyalties of pro cycling gives you a good idea of what a man is like. And Throbbo is one of the best. He was lucky. He definitely had retired. What's more, he'd found a really nice French widow who owned a café. Throbbo had been more careful than I had. He'd put aside a nice little pile, which he'd sunk into the café. And being one of those handy blokes, he's currently using his skills to extend the premises.

"Coffee and cognac?"

"That's fine, Throbbo, just fine."

It was a quiet time of day, with only a few customers. I'd come to call the place Chez Throbbo. He'd built another large room onto the existing lounge. Judging by the tools and timber spread about, it wasn't yet ready.

"Well, mate...?"

We looked each other up and down. "Well, mate indeed," I replied.

He never smiled much, and yet I'd seen that poker face creased with laughter when something struck him funny. And he never seemed to change, look older, happier, sadder. When he washed his hair it was quite auburn. But mostly, right then, he looked as if he'd just emerged from a mine. A rather pugnacious expression didn't endear him to everyone, although the lady he'd gone in with clearly saw him in a more favorable light.

"Bad, is it?" he said, sitting the wrong way 'round in a chair and resting his arms on the back.

"Well, you know the story. Nothing's changed."

"Wouldn't this Paula take you back?"

I was shaking my head while he spoke.

"She might if it hadn't been her daughter. That was a double wammer episode. Oh, sure, I was a bloody fool. But you know how it is when it comes to you free, smiling, with kind words—and there's a stirring in the under-growth."

I'd been aware of a raucous exhaust note while I'd been speaking and looked toward the street when Throbbo stood up.

"Someone you know?" I asked, but he didn't answer, instead pushing the chair aside and going to the open door. He turned. "Guess who?"

I thought for a quick second. "Not Vito Leoni?"

"None other. In that bloody Cisitalia."

Throbbo had gone outside and was waving the Cisitalia into a gap between two parked cars.

Moments passed while they stood outside talking, Vito patting the car and Throbbo peering inside.

It must have been over a year since I'd seen Vito Leoni, even then it was only a fleeting brush.

He came toward me with outstretched hand, his gleaming black pointed shoes clip-clopping on the tiled floor, a flash of pink socks, gold fillings among teeth as white as indigestion tablets.

"You old sod," I said, pumping the firm warm grip. "I thought you'd joined the monastery—Brother Vito, et-cetera."

"Not quite yet." He clicked his heels and gave the hint of a bow. "Speaking of old sods, how are you?"

He sat down quickly and we faced each other smiling. On and off I'd known Vito for years and must admit to hav-ing nursed a sense of friendly envy. The man was almost a legend and will probably be remembered long after many race winners are forgotten. For Vito had never won much during his career, which had paralleled mine. Sports writers had always found him good copy. Probably he was the last of the super-climbers, a breed that seems to have disappeared. Untouchable in the mountains, he'd ride away from the others, open up a wide gap, and then wait for them to catch up. Although a professional, he had no need to compete, coming as he did from a wealthy wine producing family. If he had put his mind to it, he could have won any of the big Tours, yet he'd seldom finish one of them. Apart from the way he played in the big Tours, his love life had been a source of speculation and interest in many a publication. He leaned across and punched me gently on the shoulder.

"Pity about your Tour. You should have won."

I shrugged. "If I could climb like you, I probably would have."

The stern hawk-like face broke into a wide grin. "I've probably lost my wings. Not sure I could pull it off like I used to. What are you, Terry? My age, pushing forty?"

I nodded because I didn't want to hear my own words. "Anyway, Throbbo, how about a bit of service. What shall we have?"

We dithered and shrugged before settling for coffees and croissants.

Throbbo regained his back-to-front chair. "Look at us," he laughed. "Prime of life they call it. More like the end of it if you ask me."

"Come off it," I rasped and Vito tutted.

"Werl..." Throbbo drank his coffee.

"Let's have a roll call," I said brightly. "Now you, Throbbo, you've definitely slung it in?"

Throbbo pulled a face as if to say maybe, although I knew he had.

"And the great Vito here." I said. "What's your position?"

"Me? My position? What can I say? The season just gone I rode Milan–San Remo and the Lombardia. Didn't push it, didn't finish either. Just keeping the hand—legs!—in. If I think seriously about it, I guess it is all over for me. I could probably ride another Tour if they'd let me and do my expected act, except that I've developed a nag that won't go away. It's a picture of not being able to drop the peloton and, if so, of being caught or even dropped." He rubbed his hands together as if they were sweating.

"So, yes, I suppose it is the end. Although I've always nursed the dream of doing what the great Bartali did three times, I'd be happy to do it once—drop the entire Tour de France on that bastard Col d'Izoard."

I knew what he was talking about, and his eyes told me he wanted to say more. To lead him in I said, "That was really something."

He loosened his collar and pulled his tie down a few inches. He sighed. "Yes, for me it's probably too late. I couldn't do it when I was twenty, thirty. Sure, I've been first over several times, but always with some hangers on not far behind." He made a clucking sound with his tongue.

The three of us had all seen the newsreels and sat silently visualizing Bartali steaming away on that damn great Alpine col.

"Anyway," Vito said, pushing his chair to one side. "Three grumpy old men won't alter anything."

He shook hands with Throbbo, then with me. I watched the slim upright figure walk away, straightening his tie as he went.

"Me too," I said, standing up. "I've got to get ready for this track appearance in two day's time."

2. My Indecision is Final

I felt a tug at the old heartstrings lining up at that track for what could well be my last race as a pro. A tug because it was the very spot where I first competed as a professional cyclist all those years ago.

Things were better then, track events pulling large crowds—crowds that are mostly back at home now watching football on TV. Never mind, there were still quite a few die-hard fans who'd come to watch. And mostly they were watching me because of that near win that haunts me. Suddenly I was a name of sorts.

Normally I could never have dreamt of pulling off a victory in such a big event as the Tour de France. I'd only found myself in a winning position because I'd latched on to a major all-star break, and all except me were disqualified for being found positive. By that I mean their urine tests showed traces of stuff that shouldn't be there.

The break had had so much time in hand that I, the sole survivor, was handed the yellow jersey of race leader.

But there was a snag to all this, and the snag was I'd been about to retire from competitive cycling, and the only reason I'd taken part was to help my protégé Romain have an easier ride down to the mountains. Romain was a likely winner, way ahead the best climber in a field of non-climbers. Yet he was a timid rider, who only came into his own once clear of the field and away on some Alpine col. And me? I was out of condition, not as young as I had been, and hadn't been training much when I should have.

The big lead I'd been handed was nibbled away stage by stage by the young hounds of hell after my blood. I didn't even make it to the finish at Paris. Sure, I got near but ran out of steam, ending up collapsed at the roadside.

So that was the reason I'd been enjoying a bit of fame. For several days, my image had filled the TV screens. Would he make it? Or wouldn't he? Financially there wasn't much in it for me. It's only at these post-Tour track events that it's possible to earn some worthwhile starting fees.

※　　※　　※

Nine laps gone. The first rider past the post on each lap got a cash prize, the main amount going to the rider first over the line on the final lap. Just in case it had been my last race, I gave it a go at winning.

A tall Dutchman had probably got the best sprint, and there was another very fast finisher present I knew of.

Quite a dodgy duo. There wasn't a lot of banking on that track. Just the same, each one of us tried to get as high as possible on it.

Swooping down from a higher position was what we were all after, as well as trying to get placed behind the leading rider so as to pip him just before crossing the line.

All easier said than done. We were all pros and had played that game before, many times. But unless you rode straight into another rider, somebody somewhere had to give.

I was reasonably high on the banking, with four riders ahead hogging the positions they'd got. To say nothing of the three behind pushing to come past like runaway locomotives.

I'd dropped a little and squeezed past the man ahead. But of course the remaining three weren't going to let me back into a higher spot. So I tried for a long sprint from where I was, with the whole pack latching on, heads down and hell for leather. Elbows either side brushed mine. The slight creaking of strained metal mixed with our breathless gasps and the yells from the watchers.

It had been close, very close, and I was given second place. Still, there were a few bucks in it for me. It was the story of my whole racing career—the thickness of a tire, half a wheel, two seconds—otherwise I might have been quite famous. No-one remembers second placers.

There was to be a similar track event the following weekend. I gave the bike a spin midweek just to keep things turning, otherwise I was letting the training run down as winter approached. There would be no road events upcoming, and probably no more for me unless I bowed to Ryan's urging me to start in next year's Tour.

* * *

Romain was in Ryan's outer office, looking agitated, crossing and uncrossing his legs as I sat next to him. I didn't want to sound too surprised. "What are you doing here?"

"They asked me—Ryan phoned—he sounded his usual happy self, so it can't be anything bad."

"He'd sound happy as he pulled the trigger." Romain hadn't had as much to do with Ryan as I had.

The secretary across the room behind her computer had developed a large right ear, so I said no more.

After a few minutes, Peter Ryan's door opened, and there he stood, beaming rays of welcome at the pair of us. "Come in, come in."

Alan Cross was there too, his small frame almost engulfed within the soft settee where he was sitting by the window.

Handshakes all around, followed immediately by coffees. Ryan's role in the team's hierarchy was mainly to do with the financial business and advertising, whereas Cross featured large in dealing with riders and their contracts. Both men considered themselves experts on the other man's job, and they'd criss-crossed so often that I wasn't sure any longer who did what.

A kinder person than myself wouldn't have described Cross as rat-faced. With his glasses on he appeared to stare, but when he took them off to scrutinize something, they seemed to dart, never still, not helping to dismiss any possible rodent family connections. Famous for hitting the bottle, the accumulated years had settled a florid hue on his cheeks. Against Ryan's false bonhomie, Cross struck you as being quietly cunning and having a brain that constantly weighed every word spoken, every movement made.

"So, Terry," Cross said. "Still pulling in the crowds?"

"Hardly that," I told him. "But not too bad. The weather's been good and that's helped."

My words were duly weighed, allowing Ryan to begin. "We've been wondering if you're still going to start the Tour, like we discussed last time. No, wait, let me finish. No-one expects you to get far, not a your age, but on the earlier flat stages you could, with a full team's support, make a break so that you're in camera as long as you could hold it. It would please all three of our supporting advertisers to see their products' names out there for much of the world to see. What do your think? There's media interest in you still."

For a moment or two I couldn't answer, until I suddenly became aware I was staring at him. He was a round man, over six feet tall, with a round genial smile and round glasses. He saw himself as warm hearted, nice but shrewd. Nevertheless he usually pre-empted all possibilities and suggestions coming from others.

"Well, Terry? You did say yes, but it's no big deal, surely? You've ridden enough Tours to know what it entails."

Truthfully I told him, "I'm still not a hundred percent sure."

My words brought up like a minor thunderclap the image of myself going down into the gutter, unable to ride another yard.

"Why aren't you sure?" Cross said, waving his coffee cup.

Before I could speak, he continued, "Your near-win was a once-in-a lifetime fluke. Like Peter has just said, you could do a lot for our advertisers. And Peter's right—you can still pull a bit of attention, as long as you don't leave it too long. You know how their minds work—'He nearly did it last year—can he do it again?' I know you can't, you know you can't. But you've got a few months of limelight left before you're…"

"Forgotten." I finished it for him, chucking in a smile.

"Well, yes. That's life. Make hay while the sun shines. It'll be good for you, good for us, good for the team, our advertisers, our image. What are you laughing at?"

"Dear oh dear." My head was shaking as I spoke. "Me being up to it. Like spinning a revolver's six chambers with one live round in it. It might work but five to one it won't. Have I got one shot left in me? Is that what you're suggesting? How the hell would I know?"

Ryan and Cross duetted a sigh.

Romain, whom we seem to have forgotten, said, "I'd love Terry to ride. He'd help me over those sprint-mad stages."

"See," Ryan said, pointing a fat finger at me. "There's the likely Tour winner wanting you there."

"And don't forget," Cross chimed in, "about this TV film of your Tour exploit they're going to make. Man, you could end up as some sort of celebrity. To have you out there, competing, in camera, speaking, riding in track events—you could be made."

Cross was showing signs of being gripped by his own enthusiasm. Before I could speak, he went on, "With a full team behind you, I don't see why you couldn't win one of the early stages. It's not out of the question, is it, Romain?"

If I knew anything, I knew Romain wouldn't know.

"Sure, maybe, why not? I'd help all I could," he said.

"Win a stage!" I said vehemently. "If I could break clear for a few miles, do you think the peloton wouldn't pull me back well before the finish. Blimey! All those sprinters behind out to collect points."

"Yes, yes," said Ryan impatiently. "I half agree with you, Terry, a stage win isn't in the cards. Father Time's against you now. I'm not belittling you, because I know that once upon a time you could have done it. No question."

Cross began clucking. "Maybe a stage win is too much to ask. Maybe it's best to think only of starting the Tour and showing yourself, collect some money, please our advertisers. Then enjoy your retirement. And we're assuming the medics are going to pass you A1. It's no secret that what's drying up doesn't show."

"Sounds like the bloody menopause," I said as everything went quiet. I took a deep breath. "If you renew my contract starting next year, would it be simply to do this Tour thing you're on about? Or would I be expected to ride other events before the Tour? If that's the case and I made poor showings, which is probable, wouldn't that dampen any Tour interest? I might do it for a one-off Tour payment with no other events."

They clearly didn't like this suggestion, although to me it made the best sense.

"Tell you what," Ryan suddenly piped up, nibbling a fingernail to conceal the smile he didn't want to give. "I've had a fax from the Argentine whatnots suggesting we send a team for a six-day track event they're holding. The usual indoor affair in a big hall. I happen to know the other teams aren't interested. Too far, too much trouble, money not brilliant, and too late in the season, just before Christmas. What do you say—you too Romain, about taking up the offer. It seems, Terry, that your few days of glory are known there, and you could well be the star attraction. Give it a whirl and then see how you feel about our Tour de France suggestion."

Outside as Romain and I headed for our cars, I said, "Have we done the right thing by saying yes?"

Romain turned his collar up. "Is it warmer there than here?"

"About the same, I guess. Those two need time to cook up something, some angle. I do think Cross was going off the Tour idea as fast as a rat up a drainpipe. But Ryan will still be pushing."

In my rear view mirror I watched Romain getting into his Peugeot. Likely he'd agree to anything as long as I was involved. If only I had his ability, his years. My head on his body, and a Tour win would be certain. To look at him, you'd write him off as a nice, fresh-faced lanky young Luxembourger, easy-going and inoffensive. But get him in the mountains, and no-one can come near him. He can fly like an eagle, always low geared, legs turning like a pair of supercharged propellers. A young Vito Leoni. Apart from Romain, there aren't any real climbers left, not like there used to be, not like old Vito. I'm told he's in Brussels, so I'd better look him up before he disappears back into Italy.

3. Life in the Old Dogs

"That's sure some car," I said to Vito as he locked the vehicle's door.

He shrugged. "Most modern cars are faster, but they have no soul."

I know it sounded like topic number one, but I was haunted by it.

"Still unsure about retiring?"

He shrugged again, opening his hands and looking at them as if they held the answer. "Not sure. And you? Still thinking?"

"They're trying to squeeze one more Tour start out of me on the strength or my recent cock-up."

He said nothing until we were inside the café. "You did well," he said quietly, leaning forward, then sitting back as the coffees arrived.

He meant well, so I replied, "Too old, that's what beat me. I guess we're both past it."

He sat thinking while he stirred his coffee. "Retire? What then? Settle with one woman? Kids? Maybe. Comfortable images to hold you in one piece. Visions of a nice dog, a boat, some rare cars, growing old together. Huh. And when you have these things you find you're—what? fifty, fifty five?" He tapped his chest with a clenched fist. "But the warrior is still there. Maybe the woman has become a nagging bully, the dog a neurotic biter, the kids out of control, on drugs or something. Your eyes drift toward younger flesh like you once had, but you have nothing to say to them.

"You're old, but the warrior won't sleep. He's all you have. He's alive inside you, dozing yet ready to stir into the man you once were, the man with a dozen willing ladies, another roaring ride up the Tourmalet, the Izoard, seeing the road rush before you as you drop at eighty miles an hour through cloud, into sunshine, the fans brushing you with admiration. The warrior, Terry, we concrete him over but he still breathes." He made a sweeping gesture with his cup before starting to drink.

Vito had always struck me as looking a bit like an Italian gangster in a film noir. He had the necessary features—a sharp Roman nose, small dark eyes which shone, radiating some unfathomable message or mood, slick jet black hair combed straight back with grey appearing at the temples.

"It sounds like there is one more Tour in you," I told him, and he smiled.

"Oh, I don't know," he let go with a stifled sigh. "And what then? Everything ends no matter how gradually we let things go."

"It's that bloody warrior," I told him while he grinned, settling back in his chair. "But the trouble is, as I've found, that having one more go might find you humiliated, beaten, and that's worse than never having known."

He pulled a face and dabbed his mouth with a serviette.

I said, "The problem with cyclists is that of all the attributes, gifts—sprinting, against the clock, puncher—climbing is the first gift to desert you."

Sighing, he looked across the street, then back at me, nodding. "I know. And that young Romain would take a lot of beating."

I told him about going to Argentina. He listened, but I sensed that my words had drifted his thoughts elsewhere and into some mythical cloud where he was climbing the Col d'Izoard. I felt he meant it, wanted it even, when he said we should meet again before not too long. He gave my shoulder another of his gentle punches. "Who knows? Perhaps we could show them there's life in old dogs yet."

"I doubt it," I said, "We'd both end up in the ambulance. No, what I want is a team manager's job."

"Don't get into all that," he said earnestly. "Take it easy, have some time to yourself, you've done your share."

Because Vito had been educated in Britain, it was easy to talk to him, so I didn't mind giving him the bad news about Paula and myself.

"Oh dear," he said a couple of times.

I thought I could fill him in and trust him not to spread it around. "Trouble is, what money I had, I put into her business."

"But she's an honest person, surely, and will return it."

"Well, I hope so. Just the same, I still have to get a job of some sort." While he finished his coffee, my thoughts flashed back to Madeline, she of the cello and big chest. Could I face it? A semi professional musician, she was the least arthritic in a quintet but would keep on singing bits of Wagner at odd times of the day and for no reason. What would I do hitched to her? Spend the winter evenings passing wind in accompaniment to her Wagner renderings? Perhaps not yet, anyway.

We spent a few minutes reminiscing about our careers, which raised a few laughs despite the fact we'd aired them all before.

We were outside the café looking over the new leather upholstery in his car, when he spoke. "I've just been thinking what you said about having your own team. Remember Corkscrew Parker? I heard he'd won that Lotto thing in Britain and he's now worth millions. Why not give him a try. He can only say no."

I had to think hard for a minute, trying to conjure up an identikit picture of Corkscrew Parker's face. It was years since I'd seen him, and at the time he was getting near to giving up the game. Me? I was just starting out. I recall he kept giving me advice, most of which I promptly forgot. "What makes you think he'd be interested?"

Vito stopped running his hand over the leatherwork. "No reason. You knew him slightly, and he's an ex-pro. Perhaps he still has an interest in the sport."

* * *

A few days later I bounced Vito's words off Throbbo, who pulled a long face. "Parker? Funny bugger, he was. He wasn't called Corkscrew for nothing. Totally bent if my memory serves me right. A waste of time if you ask me. Anyway, what do you want to get into all that team business for?"

"You're probably right," I muttered, but the thought had taken root. Ousted from Paula's, I was now living with Throbbo, bedding down in a tiny room at the back of the premises. It was not the situation that could continue, even though both Throbbo and his wife made me very welcome, assuring me more than once that I could stay as long as I liked.

With Paula I'd been set for life. Now, suddenly, I had no future that I could visualize, even assuming Paula returned my money. As it had all been lovey-dovey at the time, there was no evidence I'd ever given her the cash.

4. Don't Cry for Me

Argentina. There I was. I've always been a bit cautious about those times when everything seems to be going okay. You know for sure that something's going to come along and sock you. And it did.

When this one came, it was a big one, one I'd never even given a thought to.

Argentina was one of those places you see in an atlas, the sort of place you know nothing about and aren't particularly interested in anyway. But even there they have cycle races, and images of my near Tour win had found their way into that part of the world.

That's how I came to be there that fateful November. Somehow they'd fixed an indoor track suitable for a six-day race, one of those under-cover round-and-round affairs fought out by several two-rider teams. And mainly on the strength of me, some of our team were recruited to compete there.

After a couple of days racing around this bumpy banked track, Cross came over to me during a rest period to say that a woman named Susan had phoned several times. It was urgent and would I reply pronto, which I did, even though it meant a dash from the track to the hotel.

I hardly recognized her voice. There was an uncharacteristic breathlessness between each word as if she was reading something unfamiliar.

"Terry, Terry, there's no other way I can put this. No other way. I'm sorry. Mother's been killed. Your Paula, my Mum. Oh, Terry…"

Those few words have always stayed with me. What I said, what she said next, how long we spoke—I've no clear memory. All I can remember is a sort of buzzing inside my head.

I should have been out on the track about an hour earlier when I'd found my way back there. I guess my team mate wasn't too pleased. Despite the surrounding hubbub, I seemed to be moving automaton-like through silence. Paula's BMW had been flattened by a juggernaut that ploughed into her and several others who'd slowed down because of the fog.

The worst of it was that I had to finish the race, so I didn't land at Brussels until eight days later. I can't remember anything much about the race or Argentina, except that on the final lap of the event, in which we finished next to last, I was booed. My career could easily have ended there and then, except that the others were good about my lackluster performance, and on the face of it forgave me.

* * *

Paula's remains had been cremated some fifty hours before my plane landed which, in a way, snapped me out of my daze. Paula had no family except Susan, who'd arranged the whole funeral.

"I didn't really want you to see her," Susan said. "She was badly injured. You wouldn't have liked to see her, not like that."

Susan herself was very pale and appeared thinner than when I'd last seen her. She spoke very quietly, as if she'd been rehearsing her words, as if she was trying to telegraph something to me, something the words weren't saying. Despite her outward calmness, there was something a bit steely about the way she acted.

I gave her a long hug, which felt strange, she and I having done more than hugging. All that had eased up some time back as Paula and I moved closer to become what's now known as partners. Susan anyway was supposed to be engaged to Romain. I say supposed, because nothing ever seemed to come of it, and was only referred to in passing like a comment on the weather.

I held her at arm's length and looked into those green eyes, shining with a glow I'd not noticed before. She wasn't a particularly attractive girl, being a bit long and thin in face and body.

"I'm so sorry," I told her. "I still can't believe it. I hardly know what I've been doing since you rang me. My dear, dear Paula."

She gave me a quick squeeze and stood back, guilty perhaps because of what had happened between us.

Paula and I had sometimes talked glibly, a sort of joke, about "when I'm gone," but it's only when you come up against it do you realize what a terrible thing death is, that everything a person had and was is wiped, leaving only brief images and some photos. Already in my mind Paula has taken a small step back, and I hated myself for seeing her like that.

For the whole of December I doubt if I had more that a few full nights' sleep. A couple of times I took Susan and Romain out for dinner. Despite Romain's feeble attempts to shed a bit of cheer, there wasn't much any of us had to say. I missed that lovely lady terribly, and that business with Susan now struck me as bad.

I knew I had to bring up the subject of my money, and toward the middle of January I went 'round to see her.

Easier said than done. She'd gone away. Where? I had a hell of a job tracking her down, and I only found out where from the bank manager whom I'd previously had a few words with while waiting for Susan and Paula to do some transaction.

"Australia," he said. "Perhaps I shouldn't be telling you this."

I assured him she'd left me a note letting me know her whereabouts, but for the life of me I couldn't find where I'd put it.

But even having the name of a hotel on the Queensland Coast didn't help. Sure, she was booked in there but was always out when I rang. What's more, she never rang me back despite the messages I left.

Finally my persistence paid off, and eventually I caught her. I'd toyed with the idea of up-and-going there, but it struck me as appearing desperate. I wasn't really expecting trouble, but as casually as possible I wanted to know when my money could be returned.

I'm sure my heart lurched like a Zeppelin going into reverse when she said, "Money? What money? I know nothing about that. Mother never mentioned it to me."

This obvious lie told me what the game was and why she was in Australia.

"Susan, you know damn well that I put the bulk of my money into the business. We were living together, getting married."

With what sounded like a yawn she said, "No, it's news to me and sounds like the sort of stunt you would pull. Can you prove any of this?"

I'd already thought this would be difficult. There was no check, no draft involved. Over several months I'd withdrawn the money in cash. Being a cagey bastard and having fought a lifelong battle to thwart the income tax villains, it seemed best at the time to do it that way. And for sure Susan would have known this.

"Okay," I said as threatening as I could. "We can all play games. Now I know your attitude, I know what sort of action to take." I hung up.

The trouble was I couldn't think of anything other than physical violence.

Throbbo was all for hiring a removal truck, breaking into Paula's premises, and hijacking as many valuable antiques as possible. There may have been some logic in what he said, but with the memory of Paula still filling much of my thoughts, it seemed a horrible thing to do. And legally it would hardly strengthen my case. To confront Susan seemed to be the only thing to do. You guessed it: when I rang the hotel again, they said she'd checked out, and no, there was no forwarding address. She could be anywhere but would have to show up eventually. Thinking there might be some written evidence in my favor, I shot 'round to see what I could find on the premises. Know what? All the locks had been changed.

5. Funny Old World

It was a long shot. So long as to be almost a joke. But in my mind a mild kind of desperation had set in. What was I going to do with my life? Over the hill as far as racing was concerned, no money unless I could get my savings back from Susan, virtually unemployable and homeless. The only positive note was the few miles left in my legs.

That's why Corkscrew Parker's name kept flickering in my thoughts. Certainly it wasn't likely he'd finance a team—not a big one up to Tour standard—but a lump of money on the board could attract money from various advertisers.

It meant going to England and casually calling in on him to test the waters. The team suggestion would have to pop up like I'd suddenly had a bright idea. Funnily enough, when I got to London and put up at modest hotel, I got cold feet. Instead I began wondering if, perhaps, I could land a reasonable job and start a new life. I wrote several applications, and as money was tight, I thought I'd take a casual or part-time job while I waited.

Nearby was a big supermarket with a sign in one of the windows for someone to collect trolleys from the car park. I thought a week of that would be better than sitting around.

I was ushered into the office of the staff manager, a reed of a woman with the essentials seemingly misplaced a bit North-north-east.

"Well, now," she began when I was seated. "you say you've been a professional cyclist."

I looked at the Frankenstein footwear visible under the desk.

"And you got paid for this?'

"Sure," I told her, wondering what this had to do with retrieving trolleys. "Advertisers put a lot of money into it."

"So you—what?—rode a bike advertising something?"

The climbs around San Remo suddenly looked quite smooth. "No, no, it's a professional team. The Tour de France, all the big continental races. It's all televised. Big money."

She was putting on what she thought was a posh accent and not making a good job of it.

"Who" (she nearly said "whom") "actually pays you?"

I knew I was beginning to sweat. "Has this got anything to do with the job you're advertising?"

"Well, we have to know some sort of background to our employees, we have to know who exactly we're employing. Probably, Mr. Davenport, this is a job more suited to a younger person."

My chair scraped loudly as I got up. "I parked my zimmer frame outside. I hope it's not in the way."

So that was that. Tell any French-Belgian-Italian-Spanish-German-Dutch girl what you were, and their minds, whether interested or not, would automatically fill with various images of the sport.

To cap it all, outside as I crossed the car park, a boy was struggling with his cycle to get the chain back onto the sprockets. In a moment I'd put it right for him. "Thanks, mister. Do you ride a bike then?"

"On and off, yes."

"I bet at your age you have to walk up hills."

All I could do was smile and walk on.

I did try a bookshop where they asked if I could sell books aggressively. I couldn't suppress the grin that spread across my face as I walked out, for a moment visualizing myself pounding customers over the head with a weighty volume. I wish I'd worn a revolving bow tie and turned it into the complete joke that it was.

No, cycle racing was what I knew, and I had to find a niche in the business somehow.

Corkscrew was easy to find. Somehow Throbbo's enquiries had come up with the right address. It was a big old house in one of London's posh suburbs. The initial impression dimmed as I approached the front door, which, along with the other visible bits of the house, could have done with more that a lick of paint. I suppose the rich can afford to be like that.

He was expecting me. I'd rung on the pretense that I was in London on business and thought I'd look him up. Even on the phone he sounded old, and when he opened the door, I wouldn't have recognized him in any circumstances. A small grey bearded, bald stooped man shook my hand, saying, "I remember you. Yes, sure. A bit of a tearaway, weren't you?"

"Probably," I told him. "And how are you keeping?" I'd said this automatically. It wouldn't have taken an expert to see that Corkscrew Parker wasn't enjoying the best of health.

"Here and there, up and down." He flashed a grin exposing the gaps among his remaining front teeth.

The house was very dark and dismal, with permanently drawn curtains and furniture that didn't seem to belong to any sort of trend.

"What's yer poison?" He was standing by what appeared to be a homemade bar created from two tables and a plank of wood.

"Just a beer," I told him, and he turned away with a look of disappointment. "I'm still what passes as a pro roadman. Can't go drinking the hard stuff."

With his back to me, he said, "No, I suppose not. Be packing it in time soon, won't it?"

"Just about." At least we were quickly on to the subject. "Not sure what to do next. Something in the team line appeals."

He turned to face me, holding what looked like half a pint of rum. "Yeah, I'd thought of that too, but language was the problem. I tell you—I was at my wit's end when I packed it in. Jogged along with crumby jobs for years until God smiled on me in the form of a check."

"Lucky you. I don't have that sort of luck. Anyway, what do you do with yourself these days?"

"Not much. Got this 'orrible prostate problem. Pissing here, pissing there, pissing every-bloody-where. They sliced a bit off and said I'd be okay, but the slicing seems to have released the cancer, which has spread. I'm due for another carving soon. This time I hope it works." He smoothed a few strands of hair across his bald head.

"You bet." I'd been aware of a creaking sound from upstairs and asked him if he lived alone.

"The creaking bed springs?" He waved his glass in the direction of the floor above. "Nar, that's the missus with her bloke."

"Oh, I see," I said, hesitating. "Is the creaking sound what I think it is?"

"Ha, no, it's a recording she plays to annoy me. Oh, he's up there, but probably watching TV or asleep."

"You don't sort of live together?" I ventured.

"Oh, no, no. She and him are after me money, but I've got it stitched up so's they can't get it. He's, what? About

forty. She's sixty three. A real love match you might say."
He cupped his hands and shouted at the ceiling. "Give it a
rest. It's a waste of time there, Jack, it's like chucking a
banana across Time Square."

"That'll upset him," he said, grinning. "He'll probably
come down and start on me. Anyway, what's going on in
the big pro world. I've lost touch lately."

I'd hardly said a few words when we both looked toward
a door that was flung open. In came this tall miserable
looking bloke in his shirt sleeves.

"Enough of your bloody cheek," he barked prodding
the air with his finger. "Oh, you've got a mate here, have
you? Showing off, eh? " For a moment he quickly looked
me over.

"If you think you're getting at me with that recording,
you've got another think coming," Corkscrew piped up,
squaring his shoulders. "Shove off back to her ladyship
where you belong. You make a lovely couple."

"You short-arsed…," tailed off into a sneer, and he
came toward Corkscrew, clenching his fists more and
more the nearer he got.

Oh dear, I thought, standing up. Only been here ten
minutes and it's trouble.

"Hang on," I told the bloke, "Just take it easy. Like my
friend says—shove off back upstairs."

He changed direction and came at me, running his
tongue across his upper lip. I didn't wait to find out if it
was going to be verbal or physical.

His nose exploded blood as my right landed on target. He fell back holding his face, staggering against a chair and knocking it over. Bent double and groaning, he made for the door he'd come through and was gone, leaving spots of blood on the carpet.

"Lovely!" Corkscrew exclaimed. "Yes, I do remember you. Yes, a right tearaway. Here, what about a cup of tea and I send out for some pizzas?"

"Why not," I said, rubbing my knuckles.

Chuckling, he picked up the phone and rang for a couple of pizzas. "Be here very soon," he said. "Yes, they're up there plotting away on how to get my money, her and me being legally married. But I've got 'em beat. It's all off-shore and if they look like winning, I'll disappear pronto to some place overseas. They can have the house, but that's all. There'd be plenty left for me."

As he was talking money, I thought it too good a chance to let slip. "Ever thought of putting a bit back into the sport, seeing it's in your blood so to speak."

"Nar, not keen. It's not what it used to be. I've seen a bit of the Tour on telly. Just the same old sprint finishes. No-one who can blast the field wide open."

On cue, I thought. "Like Bartali and Coppi, you mean."

"They were real climbers. No-one could touch 'em."

"What about Vito Leoni? He'd be in their class."

"Trouble was he always buggered about. He could have won any major Tour. Mind you, if he was still riding and could do something spectacular—that would be worth seeing."

What he said was all too much for me at that moment, and I thought it best to leave the subject for a while even though the old mind was racing.

"So what have you been up to?" I ventured again.

"Here," he said, putting his glass down, "Come and have a look at my little collections." He opened a drawer and took out a bunch of keys.

"Come on."

I followed him through an open doorway into an almost dark room. He jangled the bunch of keys, selected one and opened yet another door which I'd hardly noticed in one of the darker corners. Almost immediately a fluorescent light came on, then another, illuminating the room where we stood.

"Yes, come on in."

The room had no windows. Along one wall were glass fronted cabinets full of guns while on the opposite wall hung two bicycles and various cycle parts. "My little museum," he announced. "On this wall my collection of pistols from the American West. And on the other there's much you'll recognize. Take this bike: the actual Legnano ridden by Valetti, twice winner of the Tour of Italy before the war. Like Bartali, the war robbed him of his best years and the fascists had it in for him. When the war ended, he tried an unsuccessful comeback but ended working in a factory. Just think: if you'd won a couple of Tours of Italy today you'd be made. Funny old world, innit?"

I had a good look at the cycle collection. Most of the stuff was rare or of historical interest, and I marveled at how he'd got hold of it all. But his answer was vague and I was none the wiser.

"My friend Throbbo, who you may remember, has got the beginnings of a little cycling history museum," I told him. "So what's with this gun collection?"

He puffed out his cheeks and seemed to be preparing his words. "All these types featured in the West," he announced. "Percussion Colts and Remingtons from the Civil War, among others, and these are the cartridge six-shooters here in this cabinet. Bowie knives too. From the top Smith & Wesson, Colts, Merwin & Hulbert, Forehand &Wodsworth, Plants."

"Must be worth a fortune," I commented, because it seemed to be the expected response. "Does the law know you've got them?"

"No, of course not," he said with a wave. "Once they're registered they're never really yours. The bastards can take 'em off you any time they please, and will one day. Anyway, they want as many guns as possible out of public hands. When the penny drops, guns will be man's last resort. Have you still got any?"

"Me? Just a naval Luger. I give it an airing every few years."

"Had it from your bad-boy days in Marseilles, have you?"

"That's about it. Funny you mentioning Vito Leoni. He hasn't quite retired, and I think he's turning it over in his mind about one more go at showing them all up."

He was about to answer when the pizzas showed up. We ate them in silence while he poured me another beer.

"That'd be interesting," he said. "Leoni doing a Bartali on the Izoard."

I knew I had to keep that ball rolling, even though I doubted Vito's true intentions. Besides, what was in it for me, and how did I fit in? "I think he's pretty keen," I lied, "but no Tour team would have him now. They want more than a dubious showing-off in the mountains."

"Yes, that's true." He spat out an olive stone.

I purred it out as languidly as possible. "It would mean starting a new team which included him."

His answer shook me somewhat, and I tried not to show it by studying my pizza. "And a team manager," he said. "A new guy. Like you."

"Me?" I pulled a deliberately glum face.

"That's why you're here, innit?"

I watched his beard go up and down as he chewed. How did he know why I'd come? I lolled back in the armchair. "Not especially. It's an idea I've had at the back of my mind, sure, but I never imagined you being involved. Why should you? You've got it made. Enjoy the money. You know as well as I do what running a team involves."

I felt him studying me for what seemed ages. "Tell you what. Not that I've thought it through, not yet, so don't take my words as gospel."

He said nothing further and kept on munching, so I passed a few moments looking around the room.

"Tell you what," he said again. "I've lost interest in the sport because, like I say, there are no great dramas anymore. Today, come the mountains, there's got to be one guy who's a better climber and does his stuff, but that's not the same thing." He sighed and wiped his mouth with the back of his hand. "No great climbers since Bahamontes and Gaul, and I'm including Vito because, although phenomenal, there weren't any other climbers much for him to show up. Now there's this Romain, of course, but he seems too timid."

I kept quiet and continued nodding agreement.

He pushed his plate away. "But—and it's a big but—if it all came together and Vito could do his thing, and by that I mean drop the whole bloody race, werl…"

My mind was going in all directions at once. "So to get the nod from Vito would be the first thing," I said quietly.

He closed his eyes and held the flat of his hand against his forehead. It looked to me as if he was trying to visualize it all. His head began to shake, and I realized I'd been holding my breath.

"Nar, it'd be a hell of a thing to put together. I'm not that bloody rich. There would have to be a lot of advertisers on board to share the costs. And it would have to be a damn good team with proven riders to get into the Tour. This upcoming year they'll all be booked. Next year? I might not be here, and Vito will be on his pension. So it has to be soon. You do a bit of homework, a bit of probing and let me know. But the more I think about it, the less it seems likely. With me on borrowed time, my only interest is to see Vito strut the stage. All the rest is trimmings."

He discovered a bit of pizza he'd missed and stuffed it in his mouth, alternating one bulging cheek with the other until the food disappeared in one loud gulp.

He burped loudly.

6. Middlemen

On the way back, I turned it all over in my mind from every possible angle. Expecting to have a few days to really think it through, I discovered when I got to Throbbo's two unexpected issues waiting for me. Life's like that, or it had been lately. I'd hardly unpacked my bag when Throbbo appeared, hopping from one foot to the other.

"You're here at last. How did you get on with Corkscrew?"

"Not sure. I'll tell you later. Is that letter for me?"

He tossed the letter he was holding on to the table and I picked it up. "America? Who do I know there?" A bold letterhead announced Phoenix Pictures. I scanned it a couple of times, ending with a quiet "Bloody hell."

"What is it?"

Throbbo's head was darting from side to side, so I handed the letter to him, saying, "It looks like that TV program on my Tour ride is turning into a full length movie, mainly because they've got Tom Suydam who they say here is highly bankable, showing great interest."

Throbbo looked up from the letter. "And they want you to be technical adviser. Hummm... 'For a fee to be negotiated.' But that Tom Suydam's a little bloke, isn't he?"

"When he's not standing on a box, yes. And he's to be me. Or so it seems. Looks like they're coming here pretty soon, too. Well, there's a thing. Fame at last."

Throbbo handed the letter back to me. He sniffed. "I bet they bugger it all up, even with your technical advice." He shook his head as if he'd forgotten something. "Oh, and the other thing. Romain's been trying to get hold of you. That advertising thing he's tied up in, that King of the Mountains Ice Lolly. It seems the ad agency's got cold feet because they aren't too sure that Romain will be King of the Mountains. And if he ain't, the whole thing flops."

"What's he want? My advice? What can I tell him?"

Throbbo poured a couple of cognacs and pushed one in my direction.

"More than that, I gather. I think he wants you to sort out the ad agency."

"Well, what can I do?"

"Don't ask me. Better ask him."

"I'll do that. But first a bath."

❉   ❉   ❉

"You see," Romain said at the other end of the line, "someone's been talking to them. Probably someone in the agency, someone who follows the sport, some know-nothing. I never claimed I'd be top climber in the Tour. That was their idea. We know it's likely: highly likely in fact, but nothing's guaranteed. I can't see that I'd be beaten, but you never know."

I had a mental picture of his worried face, the face he wore most of the time. "All very true, but what the hell can I do?"

"Well, you're good at these things. Would you go and see the agency and straighten them out. I get on very well with the lady there, but she's not all powerful. A strong third opinion is needed."

I didn't care if he did hear my big sigh. "But what can I tell 'em! You've said it yourself—there's no guarantee. I can't imagine what got all this going in the first place."

We went through much the same conversation a couple more times until I agreed to see the agency in question.

It was the Paris branch of one of those international advertising agencies.

The elevator whirred, Muzak lulled, and there I was in a world seemingly awash in blue denim. I'd made an appointment to see the creative director (a god, surely?) handling the project. I'd imagined flared bottoms and club feet, and I guess my eyes shone a bit when I shook the hand of Georgina Winters, a smartly suited thirty-five-year-old brunette who'd been constructed by the Almighty in one of his better moods.

She offered me coffee and I accepted. Sipping the cup, I looked over the top of it at her round beautiful face which, although it had no outstanding features, was highly photogenic.

"Yes," I began, "About this King of the Mountains business."

She held up a stop-there hand. "I'm sorry Mr., er, Davenport, but what exactly is your interest in it? I mean, are you representing Romain, or what?"

"Yes," I told her quickly, "I am representing him. As I understand it, you're hesitating about using the whole idea. Is that right?"

She gave me a quick look over. "We're having a meeting next week with the producers whether to go ahead or not. Doubts, as you know, have arisen over whether Romain can in fact win this mountain title. What are your feelings? It always was problematic, of course, but at the time if was bounced around it looked a sure thing."

Dangling earrings flashed as she reached for her cup.

I wasn't going to lie to her. "Romain's the best bet for the title, there's no doubt about that. But in any cycle race there can be crashes, the rider being sick, out of luck, such as missing a big break, punctures at crucial moments—in fact life on wheels. Nothing's for sure."

She sat twiddling a pen. "Yes," she said slowly, "My thoughts precisely. And yet on the positive side, all going reasonably well, he's a virtual certainty. And that's the bit I like. You're English?" She added this quickly as if she'd just twigged the obvious.

"Me too, although I've moved about a lot within the agency—New York, Sydney, Rome."

A little man in the back of my brain had already drummed up certain thoughts about this lady, and he began taking a step forward. Would she? Wouldn't she? I gave her a quick colorful run down on my career and was warmed by her apparent interest. We did the English-to-gether-overseas-in-a funny-country thing and had a couple of laughs. Then her mood quickly changed.

"What about these major races with mountain prizes?"

I dragged myself back from the bit where I imagined she was taking her clothes off.

"Italy and Spain. So even if Romain fluffed the Tour de France, you still have a chance from the other big Tours. I don't want to throw cold water on things, but the worst that could happen would be a crash early in the season causing him to miss most of the events."

She cupped her chin in the palm of her hand. "I thought I enjoyed Romain's confidence, so I can't imagine why you're here. Something will have to be decided very soon. I've placed a standby order for the manufacture of ten thousand little plastic racing cyclists to go on top of the choc bar. It culminates in a whirl like a mountain top."

"Myself, I'd go for it,' I assured her. "On the face of it you can't lose."

"I like Romain very much," she said quietly, "But I can't let my feelings interfere with my job."

I was getting close to asking her out to lunch, but that bit about 'my feelings' stopped me. A bad choice of words, or what? We shook hands and I kept the door ajar by saying that I'd give it all a lot more thought and maybe get back to her.

*   *   *

He'd just ridden half the Tour of Flanders course as a training run and looked pretty hot under all the winter gear he was wearing.

"Here," I said, "I saw that Georgina Winters bird. Not having a little flutter there, are you?"

He gave a silly uncharacteristic laugh and looked very guilty.

"Well, sort of. But it's all over. I've just posted her a letter ending it."

I tapped my teeth together. "Not the best idea you've ever had. She's half a mind to scrub the choc bar thing, and probably will now. I must admit I can't see you as a toy boy."

"That's the trouble, she's thirty eight. But I'll be all right. I'm a gold plated bet. Really, how can I fail? They're on to a good thing and they know it. How did you get on with her?"

I gave him a prod with my finger. "First off you're not a certainty. It's about time you realized that. You told me the deal was worth even more than you could earn in a season of racing, and that's not to be sniffed at. Gawd, if only I had the chance! And did Susan suspect any of this hanky-panky?"

"Susan? She seems to have disappeared. I guess it's all over between us. No, they need me more than I need them."

* * *

I didn't believe him, and I was right. It wasn't Georgina herself who rang him with the news, but some underling. Romain gave me a call at Throbbo's and sounded stunned. Worse, it turned out he'd taken a mortgage on a property well beyond his future means. He's okay now, but how many years has he got at the top? Maybe they would have chopped him anyway, but I couldn't help thinking he'd picked the wrong time to wave Georgina goodbye. For my part I didn't want to try filling Romain's shoes and, although tempted, thought I'd let Georgina slide. Unless of course they wanted to do a campaign around me finishing last in the Tour de France.

* * *

Vito was down in Florence and I didn't want to go there, not unless I had to. I rang the main vineyard and got shunted around until someone found him.

"Seriously," I began, "think carefully. How do you feel in principle about riding another Tour and doing your showing off act."

There was a long silence.

"I don't like my riding being called a showing off act. I may make it look easy, or at least I could, but I assure you that much training and preparation go on beforehand. You should know that. A bad choice of words. How do I feel? Well, it's hard to say. I come back to you with a question—why are you asking me?"

I realized then that I should have gone to see him, and told him so. There was a lot of background noise, and I had a picture of him holding a hand over his ear. "No, no, go on."

"Best we meet. But now I've got you, this is why I'm asking. I saw Corkscrew and it's a long story. But I think he'd put up some money toward a team if you'd do your thing. This sounds mad, I know, but he's wrapped up in Bartali's rides on the Izoard. I don't think he's long for this world and living in the past, the past of heroics and big breaks. Put bluntly, he wants to see it again before he falls off the perch. Leastways that's how I see it, even though they are my own thoughts."

It must have suddenly been a good line, because I'm sure I could hear him breathing heavily.

"Terry, he said at last, "I don't know what to say. Yes, we should meet. What about halfway, say at that café in Aix where we had those lovely fish meals?"

"Okay, how does next Tuesday sound?"

"Fine. Around midday."

*　*　*

Talk about from the sublime to the ridiculous. I heard it coming. This time it was an early pre-war Baby Fiat 500. I'd seen it before and knew its history, which simply put had it belonging to Mussolini. It was a wonder Il Duce could get in it.

Vito had to duck to get out, unwinding his legs and getting his shirt cuff caught on the hand brake.

"You want to be careful in that thing," I called out, "It must be capable of fifty miles an hour."

He seemed more concerned with his shirt cuff. "History, Terry, history," he said and slumped down opposite me, relieved to stretch his legs. I heard his knees crack. "That's better. So, do I or don't I want to ride the Tour? Think of the snags. Number one: too late to create a new team for this year, and next year will be one year too many. Number two: what riders were still going okay at forty. Not many. As with boxing, the legs go first."

My financial position was still nagging, so I was eager to push the optimism. "Quite a few were still very active in their late thirties, early forties. Plattner, Schotte, Van

Est, Poulidor, Van Steenbergen, Scherens, Cerami. And Bartali himself, who could still finish the Tour eleventh at age forty. What youngster half his age wouldn't be proud to have done that?"

He sat playing with his car keys while the waiter took our order.

"What you say is true, but which of those names were climbers? Bartali at thirty-six was still a major force in the mountains, yet he got much weaker after that. The others you named were either track stars or flat-road merchants. Most top climbers have lost it by their early thirties—Gaul, Coppi, Vietto, Bahamontes."

What he was saying was true, and well I knew it. "Forget about creating a new team. Assume we can get around that. My suggestion would be this. Stay in the race as long as you can, even if you're last on classification. Save yourself for that one big stage and try then to shake off the field. Do it on the Izoard, do a Bartali, and that will please Corkscrew and take care of what money he'd put into it. Then pull out of the race. Romain's the best current climber, and I might even have a word in his ear to ease up on the Izoard."

I felt his eyes boring into mine as if they held the answer. "Many stages before the mountains. A long, long way. To be fresh at the start of a mountain climb might be all right, but not having ridden two-thirds of the race first. Terry, I need more time, even though time's getting short."

After that we ate mostly in silence, and I could see it was all going back and forth in his thoughts. When we'd finished he said, "As for a team, I might have a useful piece of information on that. I'll keep you posted."

7. Shame About the Limp

I wasted no time getting back to Corkscrew. I was struck by how feeble he sounded when I rang him. He did raise a chuckle when he related how the upstairs lodger had informed the police about my thumping him. "I told 'em it was you who saved me, that you should have a medal. When I told the plods you lived overseas somewhere, they dropped it. They're only interested in tackling the easy jobs."

I gave a more optimistic retelling of my meeting with Vito. Corkscrew was non-committal, but at least hadn't backed away from the idea. I knew it would be useless trying to work Vito into my own team and that Ryan and Cross would laugh me out of the building. Having one crock like me was pushing the limit.

I'd not long finished talking to Corkscrew and sat juggling possibilities when Throbbo came to the back of the café and told me there had been an American lady trying to reach me. She'd rung twice.

There was no recall number given, so I waited. Eventually, in the early hours when the brain's stuck in third gear, the phone rang. It was producer Ron Metz's secretary telling me that 'most of the principals' for the projected movie were just about touching down in Paris and would be staying at the Stromboli Hotel, where I was to make contact.

I knew the Stromboli, of course, but had never been inside. It was one of those places that charge a hundred bucks just to sit in the foyer. I asked for Metz at the reception desk, and after a short wait this stocky thirty-something guy came at me with outstretched hand.

"You've gotta be Terry Davenport."

We exchanged firm manly grips and pleasantries.

"Let me look at you," he said, standing back. "That was some ride you did, God alone knows how you kept going. My teenage daughter was there when I saw the newsreel for the first time and I tell you, she was in tears."

Metz had short hair cut down to the wood so close that it seemed hardly worth hanging onto what remained, and one of those moustaches that hang over the top lip crying out for a trim. People kept queuing up behind him, hopping about looking for an opening to speak.

"You must excuse me," he laughed, "We'll get together real soon. Meanwhile mingle. Hey, there, that's Germaine Sullavan, our leading lady."

He beckoned to this striking looking woman who was helping herself to a gin and tonic from a waiter clasping a tray topped with glasses. She noticed me going toward her and made no attempt to turn away.

Being a dead original, all I could think of was "Hello."

She glanced at me before putting her glass down. "Hi."

"I Guess you're to be my lady-love in the movie. I'm Terry."

We shook hands. "Germaine Sullavan. Your lady-love. I like that. Nice and archaic. Yes, I guess I am to be your lady-love, although nothing's properly scripted yet. Tony keeps writing bits and tearing them up. Everything centres around Tom Suydam, our beloved star. My feelings are he'll end up scripting it himself. You can do that when you've got some muscle in this business."

"Don't you have any muscle? No say in anything?"

She gave something between a snort and a laugh and tapped her forehead with the palm of her hand. "Hell, no. Mine's not much of a part. I think I hover in the background looking permanently worried."

She had this way TV journalists and reporters have in camera where they move their heads and expressions imperceptibly to back an air of sincerity, concern or drama to key words. Professional speakers, I suppose. Germaine did this, did it well, and had probably done it most of her life until it had become automatic. I watched her light a cigarette.

"No, thanks," I said when she stuck a gold cigarette case under my nose. Oh, sure, she was beautiful all right. Behind the small rimless glasses her green eyes didn't blink much. She had rather a lot of hair on each side of her head, making her face look smaller than it was.

"And what exactly is your role in all this," she said, blowing smoke from both nostrils.

"I'm supposed to be technical adviser."

"Are they paying you much?"

"Not so far mentioned."

"I should get on to it if I were you."

More smoke, but she did it gracefully with a panache honed from hours in front of a mirror. At a glance I'd have said she was in her early forties, but close up I'd put it nearer fifty.

"What are you staring at?" A hint of annoyance had crept into her voice.

"I'm sorry. Watching you smoke could be a scene from 'Casablanca'."

"How do you mean? Did anyone smoke much in 'Casablanca'?"

"Probably not. It's just that you do it so well. I could just imagine you opposite Bogart."

She let go a short laugh, and I noticed the lipstick line on her bottom lip was rather smudged.

"You don't really look the heroic type," she smiled, showing her teeth were in as good a shape as the rest of her.

Meaning it as a compliment I said, "I like your teeth: wish mine were as good."

"My teeth! For chrissake! You're a bit personal aren't you?"

It looked like I'd said the wrong thing, and I began going off this woman. Best not to be overawed, so I chucked in a laugh, "I hope they're your own."

"Do you mind!" half turning, she picked up the cigarette again and pressed it heavily into the ash tray.

I felt my defenses going up. "Let's have 'em if they're false. I'd use 'em to crimp the pastry."

Hands on her hips, she moved away from me. "Anything else while you're at it?"

"What about a trumpet trim?"

"A what?"

"Nose job."

"Jesus Christ!" She walked quickly away, heading for the nearest gathering.

"Shame about the limp," I called out.

But she turned halfway across the room and smiled.

For a while I mingled, but other than a few nods and smiles made no impression, eyes seldom meeting for more than a moment. Eventually I glimpsed Germaine Sullavan coming from what was probably the ladies' room. She didn't notice my drift toward her and appeared startled when I came from behind and said, "Sorry about our exchange of words a bit earlier. Forgiven?"

"I guess so." A half smile tinged with wariness. "I suppose it was your British sense of humour we hear so much about. Frankly I can't see anything in it."

"Yet I can tell from your accent that at sometime you hailed from those shores."

With a dismissive wave she said, "Oh, way back, many moons ago. I'm an American citizen."

Neither for a moment had anything to say, and she turned away from me.

"I bet you've got some interesting stories about Hollywood," I said stupidly.

"Oh, those... Probably your cycle racing tales are more interesting. Anyway, what gives with this bike racing? I must admit it strikes me as pretty absurd, grown men riding bikes. I saw the so-called newsreel, a dim shape struggling through a blizzard. Was that really you?"

"It sure was. Yet, you know, looking back on that ride was for me a moment of self revelation."

She laughed as if I'd said something funny. "Anyway, here comes Ron. You'll be on firmer ground with him."

I only had a second to watch her heading away before Ron Metz came between us.

"Hi, Terry, great to have you here in person. We've got the makings of a great movie here right in this room." He cupped my elbow. "Come and meet some of the crew."

I shook hands with several faces whose names I promptly forgot. The star turn was clearly Tom Suydam, and Metz kept pointing him out to me until we got near the group where he was holding council. I wondered if I'd have to fill in an application form before he'd speak to me.

"He's a great guy," Metz kept telling me in a hushed tone. "Did you ever see 'The Guilt of Teresa Carlton'? Tom was nominated for his part in that movie. What a performance! And I see you've met our Germaine. There's a lady for you."

At last he cornered Tom Suydam. He came barely up to my shoulder, and I could see in his eyes what my thoughts were. Apart from a few "How do's" and a hand shake, his eyes only touched mine before he was glancing elsewhere.

8. Of All the Gin Joints in All the Towns...

I was about to tell Throbbo what had happened at the Stromboli when the phone rang. Throbbo handed me the receiver.

"It's Ryan for you." He made a pistol out of his forefinger and pretended to shoot into the phone.

But it wasn't Ryan himself, only his secretary to say they were holding a letter there for me.

When I picked it up later, I was surprised to see it was from Australia. I read it in the car before starting out for Throbbo's.

Dear Mr. Davenport,

Please excuse my writing to you. The fact is, I've read about your Tour de France exploit with much interest. As you're obviously English-speaking, I'm enquiring if you'd be available to lend some of your precious time to helping my daughter Margaret over the hurdles getting started in French racing. This for a fee, of course.

Margaret is a well-known racing cyclist here in Western Australia and is as keen as mustard to experience the real scene there in France. It's all things like licences, how to get into an event—all the problems facing a foreigner trying to make a start. I'm sure you could get her going on the right foot.

If you think me presumptuous and do not reply, I'll quite understand.

Sincerely yours,

Rose Webb

I didn't know what to make of it, and neither did Throbbo.

"Couldn't charge her much, could you?" he said from behind a cheese sandwich.

"No, not enough to improve my financial position."

"Unless Rosie herself turns out to be a bit of all right and has a bob or two."

"You're always trying to find me a rich widow," I told him. "But isn't it funny when a woman has money or prestige. I had a couple of chats with this film bird. All the time I had a feeling of knowing my place. Weird, isn't it? I shot her down a bit at first, then felt daft."

"It's the bloody class system that we were born into. I've heard of her but can't say I've seen any of her films." He started on the other half of the cheese sandwich.

"You can imagine what it's like in that business when beauty starts to fade. I might be wrong, but I reckon she must be pretty well finished with the movies unless middle-age roles come up. I don't know what age they're making her in the movie, but if she's to be in her thirties, she's not well placed for close-ups. Even this Suydam guy is in his early thirties. Too young to be me unless they plaster him to look like a Van Gogh cornfield."

After a bit of thought, I decided to give a positive reply to Rose Webb, and then wait to see if anything interesting emerged. Unlikely she'd be a millionairess. Although I needed all the fees I could get, I told Rosie there would be no charge and that I'd do what I could to help her daughter.

Meanwhile Vito hung over me like a cloud. I'd anticipated trouble trying to get him into one of the current teams. The standard response was a shaking head—even from the Italian ones. They all said how they liked and admired the man, but in the prevailing climate every man in a team had his role to play. Sure, at the last moment in a minor race he could maybe fit in as a reserve. But the Tour de France? No. I believe they all reasoned, and the same thought nagged me, that although he may still shine in the mountains, he'd fade before they were reached.

All things considered I'd had to let the Vito issue ride. I could get no figure from Corkscrew outlining the amount he'd cough up. All he'd say was "See how much is needed." If a team would accept Vito and he did his thing, the only money coming from Corkscrew would be a personal handout to Vito. And if I had a definite figure I could dangle as a bribe to some directeur technique, that could work. Things could happen, if only I had a definite figure to say, "Here's $X if you'll include Vito in your Tour line-up."

Money, money, money. It was like a vulture sitting on my shoulder. Other than combing the whole of Australia for Susan, the only thing I could think of doing was to get on my bike and keep training. But training for what?

* * *

Someone claiming to have met me at the Stromboli rang to say that Metz was calling a meeting and would I like to attend.

Half hoping I might get a cash advance, I showed up. This time it was in a private suite on the second floor. There were no media people, and most of those present were holding sheets of paper and wearing serious faces.

Metz droned on about a schedule of jobs to be done, suitable backgrounds to be looked at, and liaisons with local technicians. Tony, the writer, was re-drafting the screenplay and Tom Suydam appeared to be dozing off. Germaine kept well to the back of the gathering, said nothing, and smiled when I caught her eye. Then it was drinkies time and everyone slumped into a communal sigh of relief.

She'd been rounded up by a small group and was deep in conversation with them. Meanwhile Metz and a couple of others cornered me, Metz opening in a hushed tone, "Tell me honestly, Terry. It'll go no further than this group. Was it dope or drugs or whatever you want to call it that kept you going on that last dramatic stage? This is just among ourselves. Right?" The other two nodded.

I'd been half expecting this. "Drugs, dope, stimulants are fairly rife. There's no secret about that, although some are definite no-no's. Me? I've been tempted and can honestly say I've never indulged. And that might be the reason I've been able to continue racing up to the present time."

Metz gripped my shoulder and one of the others held up a say-no-more hand. Next he went on about how he hoped I didn't mind his personal question, but when I could, my glance swept the room to see if Germaine was not too tied up. Throbbo would have accused me of meal-ticket searching, even though my alter-ego told me this was ridiculous. To myself I couldn't come up with why I was doing this.

I was casually trying to make a beer last before being pestered to drink more, when a voice behind me said, "Well, hello again Mr. Champion Cyclist."

There she was, yet for a reason I couldn't account for, I felt a tinge of disappointment. That first impression had taken a small step back.

"How are you managing among all these men?" I asked.

"Okay, okay. I'm used to it. Usually there's a good mix, but not this time."

From what I'd seen so far, I couldn't imagine why she was there. All she seemed to do was circulate. When I asked her this, she said, "I'm here for the ride, expenses paid. I even believe Tony is trying to write me completely out of the script. But whatever, it's not a major role, and they're using my name which will come under Tom Suydam's."

I watched her light a cigarette again and had to smile to myself. She did it beautifully, and I wondered if it was for my benefit. I didn't miss the wry smile as she exhaled.

A mistake, but I found I was talking before I'd thought it through. "If you're at loose ends, I was wondering if you'd like a drive 'round, sort of sightseeing."

"That would be nice. In a day or so. I'm primed to do some expensive shopping over the next few days."

I gave her Throbbo's number. Before I left, Metz cornered me.

"I see you're a hit with Germaine, he said with a quiet laugh. "She hasn't made a movie for some years, and I guess she's a little edgy."

I felt he might want to tell me something, so I said, "She looks calm enough to me. I suppose parts get few and far between when you get a bit older."

"That's about it. It's a small part, but her name still means something. She's been on TV a few times and did a mini-series. Yes, it can get tough when the years mount up."

You're telling me, I thought.

*　*　*

In the car on the way back to Throbbo's, a feeling of depression crept over me. Perhaps it was because there had been no mention of money from Metz. And it hit me that probably Germaine was in the same boat as Vito, Throbbo, and myself—all at a turning point in our lives, all looking back at something intangible slipping through our fingers. Thoughts got gloomier and even drifted back to the comfortable, dull, solvent days with Madeline and Wagner. As the mood worsened, images of a life in Britain again came up. I did have distant relations I could sponge, although likely all they'd want were my body parts.

I'd not long been back from Throbbo's and feeling better thanks to Marie's cooking, when I had a call from Romain. The lad had an ear closer to the ground than I could be bothered with. He sounded pleased to be telling me something he knew I didn't know.

"Vito's riding in that criterium thing they hold in his part of the world—you know—that Grand Prix thing you never liked."

"Is that all you know?" I tried not to sound very interested.

"Just that. I thought you wouldn't know about it."

Yes, I was interested, but I can't think why. Unpredictable as ever, this is the sort of thing Vito did. The race was a minor affair that attracted early season starters.

I couldn't make up my mind whether Vito was using the event as a training run or if he hoped to shine in the cause of impressing some recently acquired nubility.

With two days in hand, I took off for Italy, clutching my video camera in the hope of an impressive performance by Vito, sufficient to cement Corkscrew's interest. I decided not to make my presence known to Vito, and luckily I had enough influence to cadge a promised ride in one of the attending vehicles.

It's not all sunshine down that way, and the day itself was no exception with a strong northerly wind and a burst of showers. I was late arriving for the start and missed the following cavalcade. Eventually, when one returned carrying an injured rider, I got a rear seat in a Jeep.

After a hair-raising miniature Monaco, we caught up with the tail end of the race and began edging toward the front of the other vehicles. The Jeep turned out to be carrying a couple of journalists. Eventually the driver got ahead of the race and stopped at a suitable place for photography and note taking.

It was a nasty course consisting of long stretches of switchback hills and areas of dead flat. Vito was there all right. You could pick him out from a distance. While other riders were bent over their machines, Vito appeared to be sitting up straight like a rabbit emerging from its burrow. The bunch drew near and I made no attempt to either hide or show myself. I don't think he saw me.

The bunch, which had broken from the main field was laboring hard, sweating but riding strongly. My vehicle took off in pursuit of the vanguard, stopping here and there as cameras clicked.

Came the big climb, and I was relieved to see our driver get well ahead on the gradient. There was a steep descent up to where the climb began, and with borrowed binoculars I saw his familiar figure ahead of the rest, shooting down like a CEO at bonus time toward the hairpin bend where the descent petered out. Sure, it was Vito doing what he often did, building up a lead so that he had a clear run at the big climb ahead. For a few seconds he appeared to hover on the hairpin before bursting clear.

Slowly he came into view, and he saw me as he drew near. He looked a little startled, guilty even, although all I could do was give him the thumbs up as he passed. He looked cooked, and when I saw there were still thirty kilometers to go, I did a quick assessment, which came out negative. He'd be caught well before the finish. And he was. Still, I had a fine action shot of his solo break in case I needed ammunition to prop up Corkscrew.

I hung around at the finish until he emerged showered and dressed.

"You crafty old dog," I said, doing a bit of shadow boxing.

"Ah!" He threw up his hands. "A last minute decision. I simply felt like it. Where did I come? Twelfth, was it?"

"Fourteenth," I told him.

"Not too bad then. At least I shook them off for a while."

"You're just testing, aren't you, in case this Corkscrew thing comes up?"

He took my arm and led me to one side. "Good that you're here. I have a piece of information. You know the Contra-X team has four other products to advertise? Well, Normandia who contribute nearly a third toward the cost of the team, are, I'm told, near bankrupt."

I was ahead of him. "Which means the Contra-X outfit needs a chunk of money to keep going."

"Exactly. Not that this is out in the open yet, but I'm sure that this is the case."

"Enter Corkscrew—on the condition you're part of the Contra-X mob."

He looked weary and began looking around for somewhere to sit. Once he'd found a seat, he said, "Of course there may be others, and if Contra-X aren't keen on me, they'll turn Corkscrew down. And you know, Terry, out there today I had serious thoughts about all this. I found it hard, damn hard, and for a while I definitely decided not to do it. Perhaps I am too old."

I sat next to him without speaking, then I said, "Let's go into that café and have a drink."

We crossed the road and headed for a nearby café. I was hungry and ordered French fries and salad while Vito nibbled half-heartedly at a slice of gâteau he seemed to regret having ordered.

"Don't forget the warrior," I told him. "He's not too old."

"Yes," he said, pushing the gâteau to one side. He began combing his hair.

"But maybe the legs are."

"You dropped them," I assured him, "and that's all you have to do in the Tour. Do that and pull out."

"Assuming this happens, what's in it for you?" He looked hard at me as if maybe I was keeping something from him. What he said was true, so I shrugged and kept eating. "Probably nothing," I muttered, but I did have a half-formed hope that if Vito was in, then there might be an opening for me. I knew the team manager of Contra-X and didn't think much of him.

"Don't be too down-hearted," I said at last. "Stay with it until some details and facts emerge. Keep me posted though. Meanwhile I'll nip across and sound Corkscrew out."

* * *

It was Sunday. I found him in his dressing-gown with the Sunday papers spread all around him. Once he'd shaken my hand, he brushed them all aside with his foot. "A load of old bollocks," he announced. "Here, mind that geezer upstairs doesn't see you. I don't want the plods around here."

I told him about the Contra-X team and outlined all the possibilities that could arise. He listened carefully, picking his teeth with a matchstick.

"So if Vito stays on course, are you still interested?" I asked him.

"Yeah, sure, why not. What's the geezer's name running the Contra-X mob and where do I find him?"

"His name's Garino and I'll give you their address."

"Oh, him! I remember him. Does he speak English yet?"

"I don't think so. Are you up to seeing him?"

"You mean I don't look too good?" He sat back and prodded with the matchstick.

No, he didn't look at all well, but what could I say?

"You look tired, that's all."

"Truth to tell I'm buggered. The so-called treatment is enough to kill you. But I'll get there. Don't worry about me. If Vito can capture the old days, it'll be worth every penny. Besides, I need something else to think about, some sort of interest, something to take my mind off all this." He patted his stomach and made an attempt to grin. "Funny old world, innit?"

The thought that nagged me on my way back to Paris was whether Corkscrew would be in a fit enough state by Tour de France time. There were still several months to go.

9. Catch a Falling Star

"You're only interested in her 'cause she's a film star, aren't you?" Throbbo had on his solemn face as he pulled his chair nearer to mine.

"No, don't be daft. Number one, she wouldn't be interested in me; and number two, she may well be married. Oh, and number three we might be niggling each other if together too long. We got off to a bad start."

His accusing finger loomed close. "It's the old story, people finding power or prestige attractive. Look at the famous rich old guys who pull some twenty year olds. If her name was Dolly Clacket in the local library, I bet you wouldn't give her a second thought. And…, and…, this is also true: if you made it with her, for you a sort of triumph, sort of having stripped her of all her façade. Right?"

"Right in general, but not in my case."

"It's much more satisfying bending a duchess over the kitchen table than having said Dolly Clacket in the same position."

"Oh, you are philosophical today. You've been reading books again, haven't you?"

Despite my denial, I suppose there was some truth in what Throbbo said. Yet unaccountably, I looked forward to seeing her. I suppose that, unlike Dolly Clacket, she did have an air of mystery about her, although beneath that she was probably a wreck like all of us. So I thought I'd take her for a drive and see what happened.

* * *

At the Stromboli, I bumped into Metz first. When he saw me, he crouched and dropped his right hand over an imaginary six-gun holster, as if to draw. So I did the same.

"OK, Corral, High Street, Paris," he laughed. "I'll give her a call: let her know you're here. For God's sake don't have an accident. She's not insured on this particular set-up."

This time she was casually dressed in slacks and a sheepskin jacket, with a sort of woolly skull cap on her head. Her handbag resembled a small suitcase.

She stopped right in front of me, looking me over as if I might have something behind my back. Briefly I thought she was pushing her tongue in her cheek; either that or it was bubble gum. I said nothing.

Then she spoke. "I hope you're not going to be as rude as you were the first time we met."

"I apologize. I thought you were starting to play the goddess of the silver screen."

"Me?"

"Well, it seemed a bit like it."

She wagged her finger. "Oh, no. Wrong there, definitely wrong. Anyway, shall we go? Thanks for doing this, I'm in your hands." She smacked her lips into a smile.

"No problem. And my hands are thoroughly scrubbed. What the hell have you got in that vast handbag, the head of Alfredo Garcia?"

A laugh as she swung the bag up to her shoulder. "No, you can't leave your worldly possessions unattended in strange hotels. Did you see that movie Bring Me The Head of Alfredo Garcia?"

I couldn't remember. "I may have done."

She took my arm and we walked out into the cold.

I felt her give me a gentle tug. "I heard some group may be recording a song entitled Bring Me The Rest of Alfredo Garcia."

"Dear, oh Dear." I was still grinning as I held the car door open and watched her get in, putting the suitcase on the floor between her legs.

I did the official guide act, pointing out anything that might interest her. Besides, I didn't really know what to say and waited to take the cue from her. I did the main boulevards—Montparnasse, Invalides, L'Hopital, Magenta. It crossed my mind to walk her 'round the Cimetière Montparnasse where most visitors like to go as well as the Jardin du Luxembourg. Trouble was, the weather had turned quite nasty, so I kept driving, heading eventually out toward the Compiègne Forest.

She didn't say much at all, and I wondered if she was a bit wary of me. So I pulled into a restaurant for coffee and a snack. Face to face each side of the table, I took the plunge.

"What do you think of this film, then? To me it seems an unlikely subject to interest Americans." A moment ticked by as she thought out her answer.

"I've wondered that myself. Cycle racing? The mob out there want car chases, strangulations, explosions, fucking, skulduggery among the rich and powerful. You look bemused. Isn't what I'm saying true?"

Giving my coffee a long stir, I thought before answering. "Well said. So why are you doing it?"

She held up her open palms. "Why does anyone do anything? Money, of course. Know what I mean?"

"Surely it'll hurt your career if it flops. Don't all film stars worry about this?"

"Ha! Yeah, the big stars, the current crop, they can pick and choose. I haven't made a movie in eleven years. The last one was a so-called epic that sank quicker than a boatful of holes. In it I had to wrestle with a snake, for God's sake!"

"A piece of hosepipe, surely?"

"No! A bloody snake! Actors get blamed when movies don't do well at the box office. But what can actors do? They aren't directors, they don't write the scripts. They read the lines they're given and act as best they can, as directed. Yet they get blamed!"

It was a point I could see and said so. "Metz said you'd been on TV recently."

"Two three-hour cop dramas, a nineteenth century backwoods mother, an alcoholic secretary. They've paid the bills, I guess."

Knocking back my coffee, I pointed a knowing finger. "You did a few Westerns, didn't you?"

"Several, but the genre's dead unless it's a Clint Eastwood. The old one-a-week studio Westerns now fill the gaps on TV."

With her glasses on, it was hard to imagine her out West. "In those earlier Westerns they always looked so clean, didn't they? The streets were never dusty or muddy, the heroines pink scrubbed, and the hero straight from the barber's."

She was relaxing now, smiling a lot, moving about in her seat. "Then the mud and dirt lot came along and went a bit too far in the other direction. I did one of those and had to come on the set looking as if I'd spent a week sleeping in a field, Oh..." She seemed to regret saying what she had. "... it was another age, looking back."

Leaning across the table, she began gently tapping the back of my hand while turning words over in her mind.

"Yeah, I had my own high hopes— you know, major roles, big directors. For a while things got close, then nothing. While you wait you get older, until you're past the first flush of youth. Stills from your movies decorate your room, videos on the shelf. Is it like this for you, Terry? I mean, you're not exactly starting out, are you. Metz was saying you'd never won much. I'm not trying to be cruel. Heaven forbid! But are you a second runner? Terry What's-his-name. Whatever happened to him?"

She'd stopped tapping my hand and I hadn't noticed. I looked into those green eyes as I tried to fathom what had prompted this speech. Was she telling me something or asking? I pinged her hand, still on the table, but she moved it away.

I said, "And Germaine Sullavan—where did she end up? Are we then a couple of losers? Is that what you're saying?" She dug into her suitcase-bag and pulled out a tissue to wipe her hands on. Perking up, she said with a big smile, "Every part you get could be your last, and eventually it is. Maybe this is it. A goddamn bicycle race."

10. La Vie en Rose

Back at Throbbo's, I kept turning Germaine's words over in my mind. I'd always imagined that people like her hid behind a pile of bullshit, determined to exaggerate their importance and covering up failures. Not so Germaine. Perhaps she was just feeling a bit sorry for herself. When you read biographies about that sort, they often came across as half barmy. I had to admit, though, she appeared quite calm, rattling off her theories in a matter-of-fact way. And yet I felt she was nursing some sort of sadness.

Well then, perhaps we were both losers in our own peculiar ways. More reasonably put, we were both at the end of careers that demanded youth, and that was all. Life was supposed to begin at forty, wasn't it?

* * *

I had to wait a couple of weeks before I heard from Corkscrew again. For a sick man, he could really move. He'd seen Garino and things had gone well, he said. Normandia weren't definitely out, but Garino thought it was close. Corkscrew said he hadn't mentioned conditions, in particular Vito's inclusion in the Contra-X team for the Tour de France. "I didn't want to rush things and start making conditions—we just spoke in general principles," Corkscrew said over the phone. Myself, I thought he should have mentioned Vito. Time was running out, and Vito's riding was, after all, what it was all about.

Meanwhile I had a fax from Rosie Webb. She and her daughter were in Brussels waiting to pick up a special VW van they'd ordered. Their arrival at Throbbo's was imminent.

On all fronts there seemed to be nothing to do but wait. I'd let the training slip, and as far as I knew, my Tour participation was still on. It rained most days, leaving the roads awash in some places. Naturally my machines were without mudguards, so I borrowed a small-frame cycle from Throbbo's historic collection.

Still perspiring from my ride, I went back into the house to find Marie talking to two women whom I immediately knew were Rosie and her daughter Margaret.

Big handshakes and immediate impressions all around.

Neither woman was what I'd imagined.

"I didn't phone," Rosie said. "We had no fixed address, the VW was ready so I drove straight here. Marie has filled me in about accommodation locally, and we've booked in up the road in the little hotel there."

While Marie served up coffee, croissants, and blueberry jam, we chatted over the weather and Paris traffic, at the same time looking one another over. Both women radiated a kind of honest openness, and the mother's blue eyes were duplicated onto the daughter. I found myself zinging from one wide-eyed set of peepers to another. When one stopped talking, the other took over, the subject being daughter Margaret's triumphal cycle wins. To the listening Throbbo and myself who knew, if anybody knew, what the 'route' was all about, their breathless tales seemed very naive.

Rosie was a dumpy woman with a round pretty face displaying no particularly outstanding feature, the sort of face you automatically liked and felt at ease with. Despite her lack of centimeters she was shapely, running to plumpness. In contrast, Margaret was a strapping six-footer, a kind of head girl at school, a jolly-hockey-sticks wench if ever I'd seen one. They'd left their new van, Rosie said, in the hotel car park.

"I'm so glad you've agreed to help us. Otherwise we'd be lost—especially driving on the wrong side of the road." Rosie seemed to think this was very funny.

"Mum's a driver from hell," chipped in Margaret.

"No, I'm not. A little uncertain at times, maybe. I seem to come up against some particularly dangerous drivers.

What did you think of the race photos and cuttings I sent?"

I didn't like to say I'd forgotten them. "Fine. Oh, and I have got the necessary licence forms and events calendar. You're a bit of a star where you come from, eh, Margaret? Oh, and call me Terry. Forget this mister thing."

"She's done very well, haven't you, Marg? Almost as good as some of the men."

Looking at those thighs, I found this easy to believe. "Anyway," I said, standing, "Shall we talk it over, say, tomorrow morning and nut out your plans and ideas. At this time of year there aren't any road races around here, but they've just about begun down on the Côte. I'll tell you all about it tomorrow. How's that?"

They looked delighted, so much so that I felt quite taken by their bubbling enthusiasm. It's not something that comes my way too often.

"What nice people," Marie said when they'd gone and I headed for the shower to think it all over.

* * *

They arrived soon after ten o'clock. They'd eaten, Rosie said, but I myself like drinks around when plans are involved. On suggesting tea, Rosie pulled out some herbal tea bags and asked if I'd mind her using them.

As we talked, I modified my description of Rosie as dumpy and substituted cuddly. Horrible word, but "vibrant" just about summed up the pair of them. They even sat eagerly on the edges of their comfortable chairs until I politely suggested they relax.

Rosie had one of those German helmet hairstyles, a fringe and straight down sides which swayed about as she spoke.

Margaret's wins, when described, came over as time-trialists' wins where a steady unrelenting pace might pull you clear of other riders. She was too big to be a climber and probably too much body weight to produce a blistering sprint.

They were eager to hear the story of my Tour loss, and I filled them with anecdotes on riders whose names they'd heard.

Rosie had this aura of permanent amazement and would give a single clap of her hands before holding her face, open-mouthed, wide-eyed and laughing. My tales weren't particularly funny—at least the decent ones I felt safe to tell—yet I began to feel like a comedian as the pair of them chuckled and gasped over their bloody herbal teas.

The time passed quickly and I began to feel my voice needed a rest. "So tell me about yourselves. What gives with this New Life that was on the back of your envelope?

"Well," Rosie began, edging eagerly toward me and tapping her fingertips together. "My late husband and I had this property left to us. Thirty acres and a lovely big old house from the last century. I suppose as a shorthand description we're what's now being labeled New Age folk. We've always been this, way before the term arose. Superficially we were professional people. Those careers we gave up and took over Mount Spring House. We built a dozen small A-frames, where visitors could stay when the house overflowed. We soon got going with organic food, meditation and Reiki. Both Marg and I are Reiki masters: our meditation is in the Buddhist style although we're not actual Buddhists."

I tucked all this away for future thought. "And yet you're interested in cycle racing," I said to Margaret.

"Oh yes," she perked. "Why not? I enjoy many other things also—tennis, writing, music. Mother too—she's a great horsewoman and can beat anyone at darts."

There were two women's events down south. To my quick suggestion and surprise that they go for these, the pair of them bubbled over. Time, however, was pressing for me, and I was already wishing I hadn't got too involved with Rosie and her daughter.

11. Best Laid Plans

I still couldn't make up my mind about the pair of them. They were so bloody nice. I find it a bit hard coping with people like that. Often it's a mask for a much blacker personality. Yet if they were genuine, then their enthusiasm was welcome. They were going to need it.

I wanted to stay close to Throbbo's, in case there was good news from Corkscrew. Luckily I had a contact, Yves, down south, so I buzzed him and he agreed to do the necessary arrangements for Margaret. Before they left, I told them to really familiarize themselves with the 57 kilometer road event that Yves had recommended. I gave Margaret's machine the once-over and waved them goodbye, saying I'd follow in a couple of days if events allowed.

Lucky I waited, because Corkscrew rang to say that Normandia had definitely withdrawn and that he was going to see Garino again about Vito's participation. I wanted to be in on this and I told Corkscrew to include me in the meeting with Garino.

Yves had everything in place when I arrived. Rosie bounded out of her hotel, taking my hand and giving it a good shake.

"We've been around the course a dozen times. Yves has been wonderful."

"Only two days to go," I reminded her.

"Margaret is out all the time, getting the miles in. Do you think, Terry, she could win?"

"I shouldn't go counting on it. This is just a trial to see how she gets on. Me, I want to have a doze; I've been driving all night."

"Would you like a Reiki? You know, a Reiki, what Marg and I do. It'll relax you wonderfully."

I didn't know what to say. "Well, I'm not sure. What do I have to do?"

"Do? Oh, nothing, just lie on the bed and leave the rest to me."

"Aye, aye, I know your sort."

She slapped my hand. "Naughty boy. It's nothing like that, not at all. Reiki is a universal life energy, it accesses the mind, body and spirit and accelerates the body's natural healing. Me, as a practitioner, all I do is place my hands in a sequence of positions on the body. Most people experience deep relaxation. By the look of you, that's just what you need. You'd like it at our place back home. Perhaps I can persuade you to come sometime. Meditation too can be wonderful."

"That place of yours—it's not all tree-hugging and ene-mas, is it?"

"No, no, of course not, heaven forbid!" Whatever her lifestyle involved, she certainly appeared to have radiant health.

I said, "I did do meditation once. Life came along and swamped it, and I guess it just slipped away. I remember years ago, when I was on this big team, there was an end-of-season get-together in this hotel. We had to share two to a room, so finding somewhere to meditate was very dif-ficult.

The rooms weren't en-suite, but there was an extensive toilet on the same floor. To get on my own, I went into one of the cubicles and shut the door. Just getting started when someone came into the adjoining cubicle. He must have come from a curry conference, because he nearly blew me out of my cubicle. Gawd! It was like The Charge at Feather River."

This really tickled her and she couldn't stop laughing. "Dear oh dear. I've heard of difficulties being placed in the path of meditators, but..."

Right then she looked so cuddly that that's what I al-most did—cuddle her. But something checked me.

* * *

Thirty five starters, fifty-seven kilometers, fairly flat course. A horde of lovely young women, ablaze in well-fitting colors, one of them about double the size of the others. She could have cracked walnuts between her knees. Immediately I thought of her as the Soviet Tractor Hero. A wave of the flag and they were off, Margaret just visible in the middle of the bunch. The Tractor Hero grabbed my attention. In no way could I see her getting anywhere in this race, a suspicion that soon came true. Some 20 kilometers out, and she came back on her own, freewheeling slowly, flushed and sweating. I asked Yves about her. It turned out he knew her and her family. She was, he said, the local track star—too heavy and powerful for the road, but blessed with a withering sprint.

About forty-five minutes later the bunch reappeared in the distance, heading for the finish in one solid group. Long hair flowing beneath crash helmets, pink gasping faces, they charged for the line. Near the back was Margaret. I caught her as she freewheeled in, out of breath and trying to smile.

"You did fine. It's a start, a learning experience I think they call it now."

Between gulps of orange juice, she shook her head, taking a sponge from Rosie to wipe her face. "I tried to break out, but they just sat on my wheel. What else could I do?"

"Next time you'll do better, won't she, Rosie?"

❖   ❖   ❖

Next time, yes. The same thing was certain to happen. A plan had begun stretching its legs inside the old brain-box. So I asked Yves to introduce me to the Tractor Hero, whose name he said was Lisa. Not a word of English was known to her, so our conversation was in French.

The next event was similar to the first, but slightly longer and hillier. No, Lisa had no intention of competing; the road was definitely not for her.

Out of parental earshot, I peeled off the equivalent of two hundred bucks. I told her that all I wanted her to do was enter and sprint away right from the start, ride as far and as fast as she could, then pull out. Why? Because the Australian girl would go with her. No other rider worth her salt would go with such an early break, especially as she, Lisa, had proved she couldn't last—and because Margaret had come in near the back. Neither looked dangerous.

Sheepishly, looking cautiously around, she took the money. A quick handshake and we parted.

An hour before the race and feeling good from Rosie's Reiki, I took Margaret to one side.

"Listen. I have it on very good authority that the big girl, Lisa, is going to tear away as soon as the flag drops. She has no intention of finishing. She's doing it partly to show off to some boy and partly as a training exercise. You, dear Margaret, must go with her. You must. Once Lisa's had enough, you'll be on your own. You're good at the solo plod. Forget what's coming up behind you. Ride like in a time trial, but go with all you've got. With luck you might just make it to the line on your own. If you don't, and you're swallowed up, at least you'll have had a lot of exposure, and I'll make sure the cameras click, your mother's movie camera too."

She'd been frowning while I spoke. After a couple of unfinished attempts to ask questions, she said, "Okay. I suppose it's my best chance."

Yes, I felt a bit smug when my plan worked. Even so, it was a close call. The pack nearly caught her, but I could see she was going to make it. I've had a few packs after me in my time, not counting the income tax people. It looked like they were moving at twice Margaret's speed. Good girl, she hung on, looking all in, head swaying, those big thighs almost crying out for a rest.

I arranged a victor's bouquet, and wreathed in smiles, she rode up and back in front of the spectators.

Rosie hugged me but let go a bit smartish when I kept it going too long. I took the twenty-exposure film from my camera and handed it to Margaret. "There, for posterity, your first win."

I couldn't hang around much longer. There were no more suitable events for Margaret, not for three weeks, and Yves said he'd do all the necessary. Meanwhile Rosie reckoned they'd tour around and see the sights. Before leaving, I rang Throbbo and asked if he'd look after the women's interests while I was absent. Inexplicably I wanted to see Germaine again, even though there was not time for that, especially as Throbbo told me there had been a call for me from a Michael Padovkin 'to discuss a business matter'. That was all the man had said, leaving his phone number for me to make contact.

Driving back to Paris, I kept running my future over in my mind. All the way I had this here-we-go-again feeling that wouldn't stop. Soon, if I didn't get something, what sort of future was there? If only I could have got hold of Susan.

Women? I was too long in the tooth to appeal to passing nubility, or them to me (what would we talk about?). Guys my age with slender wallets—what happens to us? I've seen some go half barmy and hover between extremes as different as socialism and sodomy.

And who the hell was Michael Padovkin?

12. Vélos Mickey Mouse, Moscow

I soon found out. In broken English he described himself over the phone as a Russian designer of a revolutionary racing cycle. Fine, I said, but where did I fit in? I gathered he knew about my Tour ride, which seemed to be all he did know of the Tour and mistakenly thought I was some sort of big-name champ. Without wanting to run myself down too much, I made it clear that I was a well-known team man with various contacts within the sport. But that was all.

It turned out he wanted me to use my imagined influence to get the team I was in to use this wonder cycle in the Tour de France. The kudos from this would be the best advertising he could possibly buy. I told him he was wasting his time. That is until he offered me thirty thousand US dollars if I could pull it all together. More out of curiosity than anything else I agreed to meet him at the hotel he mentioned.

Without being too unkind, Michael Padovkin looked like, and even walked like, Groucho Marx. Large block heels on his shoes, put there to increase his height, gave him the appearance of a man walking permanently down hill. To top it all, he even had a black moustache. I found I couldn't stop grinning, which he took to be affability on my part.

He was accompanied by a very fat lady, introduced after much hand shaking as Gloria. There must have been a mix up at the christening to land her with an unlikely name like that. She at least spoke better English and hovered around us in the dimly-lit hotel room, ready to correct or translate.

"You see, Mr. Davenport," Padovkin said, "Our design is quite revolutionary. In a moment I will show you why. To have our machine in the Tour de France, let alone be ridden by a winner, would ensure our immediate acceptance and secure substantial sales throughout the world. For this reason I am prepared to pay you the sum mentioned."

"Just how successful would it have to be for you to pay out that sort of money?" I asked this while not quite believing my ears.

Big Gloria spoke. "Getting it in the Tour, that's all. That would be sufficient." In spite of her visible tonnage she had a squeaky singsong voice.

As if he was about to conduct an orchestra, Padovkin bowed, then pushed aside the big sofa. And there it was. He wheeled it out and leaned against it right in front of me.

"Okay," I said, slowly standing up. "So what's so special?"

Gloria jumped in. "You will observe that the frame tubing is much fatter than usual." She squatted down accompanied by a creaking sound, pointing to the bike's lower half. "And the whole bottom bracket is very much larger also."

Images of Vito and Throbbo rolling up with laughter danced before me. "It must weigh a ton," I commented, trying not to grin.

Gloria picked the bike up as if it had no weight at all. "See for yourself." There was a hint of smugness in her voice.

So I took the bike from her. Yes, I was surprised. It was no ultra lightweight, but nevertheless it weighed little more than the average racing cycle.

"You look impressed," Padovkin said.

"Sure, it's much lighter than it looks." I pushed my foot against the fat bracket. "And it's quite rigid," I had to admit. "But what gives with this fat bracket business?"

"Ah!" he said, stepping in front of Gloria. "This is what makes it unique. You have noted the triple chainwheel. Well, inside the bracket's casing is a preselect gearbox which, combined with the chainwheel, gives twenty-one ratios. So the rider can select the gear he wants before he needs it. A light miniature battery and cogs of the lightest, hardest steel are the secret."

I went through the business of examining the machine and although it was, well, interesting, I could see no advantage over current racing machines.

And yet... Thirty thousand big ones. That part of the brain that can really work fast in emergencies came in strong. Certainly the machine had no chance of acceptance. But what if I genuinely tried to place it—just as long as I had a cash advance to see me on my way. Say fifteen grand?

"I'll be honest with you," I began. "To replace existing machines would be very difficult. It would take a lot of time and effort on my part. But if you could show goodwill by advancing me a sum of money, then I'd do my best to work for your interest."

We went all 'round the houses, neither party willing to come forward with an actual amount. Finally I tried for twelve grand but had to settle for ten.

He disappeared for about fifteen minutes, presumably at the hotel safe, and put the ten grand into my increasingly moist palms. Lovely to be solvent again.

He waved aside my suggestion of some sort of receipt. "You are too well known to practice underhand dealings. Besides, I know you to be a man of courage, which is why I approached you."

Chapter 12. Vélos Mickey Mouse, Moscow

With the front wheel removed, I put the machine in the back of my car. Padovkin was staying indefinitely at the hotel and he gave me his mobile phone number. I stopped at the bank on my way back to Throbbo's and changed the US dollars. As I drove along, I kept patting that lovely bulge in my jacket pocket.

* * *

"Mickey Mouse!" Throbbo picked the bike up, put it down and walked 'round it. "Stone me. I hope this isn't 'another fine mess', what with trying to get Vito to create history and Susan scarpering with your money—to say nothing of Rosie and the film star. Why can't you lead a normal life?"

"Why indeed. The ladies you mention are no problem, not yet anyway. Susan I must eventually catch up with. Vito's on course, almost. And the wonder bike? I know it hasn't a chance in hell, but I'm keeping my part of the deal."

Throbbo cupped his ear. "You don't have to bother showing the bike to anyone. Just describe it. I can hear them laughing already."

He was dead right of course. Ryan and Cross both looked at me as if I was mad. Luckily I softened the impact by openly admitting there was little if any advantage in Padovkin's cycle, and I was doing it to oblige the man.

"I promised the guy I'd show you. I'm just doing him a favor. As you say, a flat battery on the Col de Tourmalet would be no joke." I joined them in a malicious chuckle.

As for the few others I had contact with, I came away with the impression they thought I was a candidate for the male menopause.

Still, I had money in my pocket, the attention of two women, and Vito's likely participation in the Tour de France. What's more, I'd concluded a deal with Ryan and Cross regarding my own appearance in the Tour. And I eventually persuaded them to forget about my riding in any other event unless I chose. This for me was the important bit. There comes a time when you've had enough even though there would still be plenty of pre-Tour training to be got through. I guess subconsciously I'd give Padovkin a rest and let him assume I was knocking on doors on his behalf.

Garino of Contra-X was the remaining obstacle. A dour man with little English or French, I had a feeling he would be a hard nut.

*   *   *

I picked Corkscrew up at the airport, stopping first at Throbbo's. The two hadn't met for years and I left them to reminisce while I changed. Corkscrew still looked rough and I wondered yet again if he'd by okay at Tour de France time. When I'd found the Contra-X office, I parked the car and went in. We were expected. After coffee and gateaux, we got down to business.

"Monsieur Parker has told me that a condition to his financial input consists of Vito Leoni being part of my Tour team." He had a potato type of face, unsmiling, pausing over the heavily accented words.

I kept quiet and let Corkscrew say, "Yes, that's about it."

Garino placed his finger tips together, carefully, and sat back in his chair with a look of incredulity on his face. "Why, pray, is this? The man is a clown. Worse, he is an old clown. He could make my team the laughingstock within the sport."

I'd definitely gone off Garino. Corkscrew was waiting for me to speak. "This may seem strange to you. And, true, it is. But let's just say that we have our reasons. I can see that Vito's participation virtually reduces your team to eleven riders. I don't believe Vito's much of a team man unless they're all working for him. Even so he'd be no actual hindrance and he'd draw a bit of attention to the team. How you'd justify his presence to the media I do not know. Some yarn about a last minute replacement, I guess. So you start the race one team man short, but if there're no more offers of finance then you don't start at all."

I could almost hear the old grey matter going around in his head. Silently he offered the plate of gateaux, first to Corkscrew, then to me. He downed some coffee before saying, "There may be other parties interested, parties without conditions."

I knew this to be true, and it was a factor we could do nothing about. We went through it all again and left it that he would contact Corkscrew within the next couple of weeks.

I'd only been back at Throbbo's a few days, mostly spent trying to find a way to see Germaine again, when I heard from Padovkin. He said he'd rented a small warehouse and had some of his wonder cycles due to arrive. I told him he was jumping the gun and that I'd had no luck interesting anyone. He didn't sound, however, in the least concerned. Probably placing a few machines as novelty cycles for the general public was the best he could hope for. To keep my end up, I'd best show a bit of interest and call at the warehouse to look the cycles over.

I kept Vito informed about Contra-X and was glad to hear that he was still expecting to ride.

When I came back from a fifty kilometer training run, Throbbo was outside on the pavement clearing a table.

"That film star bird rang. Can you give her a buzz."

I didn't show it, but I felt quite elated. "Thanks. Did she leave any message?"

"No. She said you had the Stromboli's number but I wrote it down in case."

13. The Way We Were

First I had to eat, drink, and have a bath. My usual before going into battle. It felt like I'd been driving that car for weeks: being stationary was temporary bliss. After a couple of hours recuperation, I picked up the phone. "Germaine?"

"Terry, you got my message. How are you placed tomorrow evening?" She had one of those appealing American accents.

"I'm free. Why, what's up?"

"Oh, nothing much. It's just that one of my movies is on TV at 6:30. Egocentricity ensures I'll be watching. Care to share this unique once-in-a-lifetime experience? Or, of course, you could just as easily see it at home."

I knew Throbbo would be hammering or painting somewhere and Marie busy in the kitchen till late. Anyway, Germaine's invitation was appealing. What rude remarks could I come up with? "Can I park at the Stromboli?"

"Yes, of course, there's a block of spaces reserved for us, and most of the others will be out doing what they shouldn't."

"Okay, about five or five-thirty?"

"Fine, see you then."

The Stromboli had the air of a deserted fort, the floor she was on even more so.

"Ah, you're early. Come in." Light grey slacks, a top with zig-zags going in all directions, hair a little on the wild side. For the first time I noticed those eyes behind the glasses didn't blink much. Movie training, no doubt.

"Greetings, O celestial radiance. How are your gum boils?"

She poked a finger at me, pistol like. "Don't you start."

I moved to give her a hug but she turned away and didn't appear to notice. "So, it's like the morning after the night of the long knives out there. Where's everyone?"

Her eyebrows shrugged. "Perhaps they've gone out anywhere to avoid seeing my movie. Who knows? Now what would you like to drink? They provide the necessary here in the rooms if it's only tea or coffee."

"I'm fed up with it but coffee'll be fine."

She went into the corner of the room where the drink making gear stood. For sure she had a great figure and I took the opportunity to study it.

"Shall I do the coffee the way you limeys like it—stewed, weak, in a paper cup?"

"As it comes. Frozen on a stick if you like. I suppose we ought to stop being rude to one another. Truce?"

She looked over her shoulder and laughed. "Truce or surrender?"

"Neither. I had my fingers crossed."

The coffee ready, she turned and faced me. Why had she asked me there? See my movie? Come up and see my etchings? Surely not.

"What's the film called? And is it your personal best?"

A thoughtful pose, head on one side. "Middle of the road. I made it sixteen years ago. It's called The Long Path to Nowhere."

"Was that when the world was round and your path strewn with roses?"

"Something like that."

As she put the coffees down, I said, "It's a cow, isn't it? The passing of time."

Sitting opposite me, she said, "Sure is." Rather furtively she took her glasses from her bag and put them on, embarrassment showing in her smile. I found they suited her. "That's better. Something for me to breathe on."

She sat up straight as if to say you should be so lucky. "I suppose you're the standard British fornicator?" Her words dissolved as she ran her tongue behind her teeth.

"On and off, with taste."

"What does that mean?"

"I usually keep me socks on."

"Huh. You know, when I first saw you, I was reminded of a used car salesman. Were you ever one?"

That stung me a bit. "Truce, remember? No news on the film, is there?"

"Truce, Okay. The trouble with Suydam is that he wants to write the script himself. He and Tony row all the time. Tony's not a bad guy, but Suydam is terrified of making a dud. He's pushing for a scene where, at the end, he drags himself or I drag him all bleeding, through the mud lugging the bike as well. At the finishing line a glamorous young woman, his true-true love awaits him. Me? I'm in the background biting my knuckles, turning away through the storm knowing I'll never have such a wonderful man for myself. If Suydam has his way, I don't even speak in this movie. Just hang around in the wings with a long face. Left to Suydam, I'd work in a scene where he wrestle with the creature from the black lagoon."

"I see," I said, meaning I didn't. "It sounds like it'll sink unless Suydam gets his own way."

"That's what I'm beginning to think. Metz only got the finance to probe locations, get some background footage to show the backers in L.A., and check out Suydam's reaction to the whole feel for the story. No Suydam, no movie. I wish my name was still big enough, but those days have gone. I'm involved only for the money, peanuts though it is unless the movie eventuates. I'm really here because it's a paid-for trip. If it hadn't been for this, they might have found my remains bricked up in Alan Ladd's old dressing room at Paramount."

I put my hand out and she took it, giving it a little swing before letting go. She said, "I guess you've caught me at the end of things."

"What things?"

"Just things. The twilight of the gods."

"How many times you been married?"

She clasped her forehead, waving her hand dismissively. "God! You shouldn't ask. Three if you must know. And I still am."

That was a surprise. "You still are? Who's the lucky guy?"

"Who indeed." There was a long pause while she sat there with her eyes closed. "You wouldn't have heard of him. He's very rich, older than me. Owns property all over. Wanted me to show off to his buddies—'My film star wife'—you know the scene." She stood up quickly, clearly agitated. Turning, she said, "I've lived my own life for about the past six years. Every now and then I get a few breaks, a few parts." Both her hands went up to signal she'd said enough. "The movie. Let's get settled. Do you like chocolates?" She produced a box of walnut whips and stuck them under my nose.

"No thanks, I have to watch what I eat. Just lately I've drunk too much coffee."

She pulled a long face. "Oh, dear, what a dull life."

"Okay," I said and took a couple of chocolates while she settled herself next to me on the sofa, putting the walnut whips between us. A flick on the remote control and the TV screen lit up.

"The lobotomy box," she said.

"Germaine—why did you ask me here?"

She wrinkled her nose so that her glasses slipped. "I dunno. Not why you might be thinking. You're a tosser really, yet I can talk to you when you're not being rude. Anyway, look, the twinkling screen is about to reveal all."

Ignoring what she'd called me, I felt the stirrings of an emotional twinge as the words Germaine Sullavan filled the screen. Shooting her a crafty glance I noticed a tightness had crept into her features and she appeared to be holding her breath. All understandable, really. Sixteen years back I bet she'd never imagined sitting next to a tosser car salesman watching it in a Paris hotel. What was she then? About 38? Well worked over by studio makeup artists, she was, I had to admit, a bit of all right.

An hour and a half went by. Luckily it was in English with French subtitles. Methodically and evenly paced, she ate all the chocolates. Mid-way through she'd dimmed the lights. The movie was okay, fine, even though I prefer them with more action. This one was about an attractive middle-class family whose son is kidnapped and despite the pursuit of all suspects, it turns out a distant relation was responsible. There were a few love scenes and a couple of minor gropes, all faded out before too much of Germaine was exposed.

When it finished she still sat there, turning the set off and not moving, eventually facing me, not shy to hide she'd been crying. We touched hands again. "The way we were," she said quietly, then stood up, turned on the lights and said, "More coffee, or tea this time? I could send for some real booze. You do drink real booze sometimes?"

"Okay, what about some port? I like port. Tunes up me old gout."

"Port!" She gave a ladylike sniff. "Right, I'll send for some."

Eventually it arrived and I had a struggle uncorking it. I could see she didn't care much for it.

"Hey, she said, "I bet you've not seen any cash from Metz yet?"

She stared knowingly at me when I said I hadn't. "No, it figures. Suydam'll write the whole damn thing, make it like he wants. We're all redundant. You're the guy who can tell it like it was, but has anyone asked you? Showbiz dreams! The weirdos are becoming the norm."

"Sounds like we're in the knacker's yard of hopes," I muttered with a nod.

She put her port glass down heavily, hinting she didn't care for it. "Oh, it's the on and on-ness of it all, this damned life, where the talentless, worthless and criminal are rewarded. I suppose I'll end up going back to

Paul—that's my husband—simply for the financial freedom it would mean. Become the smiling hostess again."

I knew the traffic would be heavy getting back to Throbbo's. A quiet sigh and I made getting ready to leave movements. "Well, best be off. Many thanks for letting me see the movie. It was good, honestly, and you were great."

"Oh, thank you. Sorry I called you what I did. It's not a word I like."

"And a car salesman?"

"Yes, that too. You're the nicest guy I've met in a long time. Better go or I might get weepie again."

"Don't be late for choir practice."

She came close and kissed me on the cheek before closing the door quickly.

14. Rosehip Tea

"Tell me about this thing you're involved with, getting this Italian to do something extraordinary in the Tour de France."

Rosie's hotel was a couple of hundred yards up the road from Throbbo's and I'd gone there so I could talk to Rosie in peace and quiet.

"I like your wording—'something extraordinary'. Although in a way it's quite accurate."

Rosie appeared to have visited a hairdresser, because her earnest face peered unblinking from within a mass of curls. "Accurate but not accurate—how do you mean?"

"Looked at reasonably it's very far from ever happening," I told her. "I'm involved. I'm the instigator, but there's nothing in it for me."

She patted one of the new-found curls. "So why have you done it?"

The hotel had supplied Rosie with a teapot and cups, all set out with biscuits on a very colorful tray. She poured slowly, looking back and forth between the tea and me.

"I often ask myself that," I said cautiously.

While we drank, I gave her a potted yarn on how it had all come about via Corkscrew and my search for a team manager's job.

"How strange," she said a couple of times. "What will it actually prove—that is, if you are trying to prove something."

"You know, it's funny, but I can't tell you why I have pulled it together. Yet somehow it's because it's important, like writing The End to something, something final that has to happen. Maybe something Corkscrew said sparked it off. He said it was more than a rider dropping the whole field, because Vito's done that before. He said it was something almost magical. He's kind of right, too. And yet it could all easily fail. Even if it gets off the ground and Vito can stay in the race, he himself may be ignominiously dropped. If it works, it'll be more than a mountain duel. Perhaps magical is the right word."

"Umm..." she hummed thoughtfully. "I must say I can't quite see it in that light no matter how dramatic it might be. Here, look, I'll show you the snaps I took of Margaret's race last week. She's a marked rider now and couldn't get free, finishing twelfth."

Rosie stood up and went to her handbag. I watched her, sensing a slight grin as through her skirt she gave one side of her knickers a gentle tug where they had ridden up into an uncomfortable position. She had nice legs, but being short the skirt itself needed to be a bit longer.

I don't know why I said it but I did. "Rosie, are you married?"

She paused, opened her bag and took out the photographs. "Here, this is a good one. What they call a fine action shot. Yes, I'm married. And if you must know it's on shaky ground."

"And why's that?"

"How shaky, you mean? His name's Norman and he's having an affair with the woman who owns the local health food shop."

She didn't seem put out by my questions. "And you're thinking of ending it? The marriage, I mean."

She shook her head, implying she wasn't going to answer that one. "You mentioned once that you've met this Germaine Sullavan. What's she like? Glamorous, I suppose?"

"No, not really, not like you might think. She's got sort of bushy hair and wears glasses." I was quick to realize how automatically I'd played Germaine down to another woman, and then almost blurted out "Even so she's a bit of all right."

"Truth to tell I may leave Norman once I can see my way clear to wrapping things up amicably without feeding the legal system."

I suppose I was expected to say "Sorry to hear that," so I said it.

She flicked her wrist as if to brush my comment aside. "No need to be sorry. Margaret's now of an age where she can lead her own life, although I'd still help her out if I could. She's doing well and should get her degree. After that—well? Who knows? Now, what are your plans apart from this mountain thing?"

"Plans? I don't really have any." I told her about Susan and my hijacked savings and she listened intently.

"You say there's no actual proof you gave Paula the money? Oh, dear. No wonder your future's a bit uncertain."

"I can't see beyond the Tour de France. There's my own one-stage ride to get over followed by Vito's affair. I have to keep an eye too on Romain. He's favorite to win the Tour, but I like to see he doesn't do anything daft and spoil his chances. He's training like mad, and that's what I should be doing very shortly."

She sighed. "We all seem to be at a point in our lives, don't we?"

I hadn't intended, but found I was standing and going to where she sat. She didn't resist my kissing her and after a while responded strongly. And for the first time in my life I took matters no further. Why? Because the last woman I'd kissed was Paula and I still hadn't got over that.

Just as well, because she gently pushed me away. "I'm not quite ready for that, not yet. I need to know you better."

The push lingered as if uncertain to become a tug, so I took her hand away and patted it between my palms. "That's okay," I said, "Forget it."

"No, I won't forget it. It was nice. But not yet. Let's see if there's any more tea in the pot, shall we?"

"I should be going, I told her, but sat down again when I saw the disappointed look on her face. "Okay, tea it is."

She straightened up and smoothed her dress, putting on a big smile. "You said something on the phone about this new Russian bike. Margaret would be interested."

"Oh, that. No, it's a non-starter, a gimmick really. But Padovkin—that's the bloke—seems to think it'll sweep the board and now tells me he's taken a small warehouse and brought some cycles or frames over here already. It's a waste of time trying to interest the racing circles. But he's given me a retainer fee, so all I can do is try some of the ordinary cycling outlets. That's where I ought to be this afternoon, looking at the stuff he's imported."

So I stretched the tea-party to a reasonable length before taking off. I half regretted what had happened between us, but what was done was done. I'd told her I wanted no fee for doing what I had to fix Margaret up, and I was beginning to wonder if she thought I'd done it as part of a softening up process.

* * *

I was a bit late arriving at the warehouse. Padovkin and Gloria were already there, he smoking a pipe and Gloria pacing up and down.

"Have you no good news for me yet," he asked straight away.

I told him the truth and listed the few possibilities I'd tried, albeit without hope.

He tutted and bit on his pipe.

Having already had a good look over the sample cycle there was nothing much further I could do there. There were only a few basic frames. I picked up a couple and pretended to look interested. "Why are the main tubes bolted together and not welded or lugged?" "Ease of manufacture and to hold down the price," Gloria piped up. "Also a damaged tube can easily be replaced."

I suppose that made sense, as if anyone cared, but I gave an enlightened nod of approval.

I had to reel off some hurriedly made-up comments supposedly coming from those I'd approached, all far from the truth. Padovkin looked agitated and tired, so before I left I stoked the fire of hope by saying there were several more possibilities I could try which had just occurred to me.

So I tried all the larger cycle outlets. A couple said they'd take a few of Padovkin's wonder bike 'to see if there was any interest'. I left it like that because Padovkin and

Gloria had returned to Russia for a while. Not, I hoped, to bring back more cycles.

Being urged by Romain to accompany him on his training runs, I finally convinced myself that this is what I should be doing. What capped it was a call from Vito saying he was fed up training alone and could he join us. At this stage it was a matter for all three of us to get in as many fast miles as possible. Hills would come later for Romain and Vito. Romain, anyway, was already competing in some early events.

Belgian drivers are reasonably sane, so after I'd met Vito at Brussels and joined up with Romain, we decided to load the cycles into the team's van and head for the western side of Belgium. A nice hotel at Poperinge was known to all of us and we made this our headquarters, somewhere to eat and sleep. Daily and with little variation, we'd do a jagged circuit taking in Wevelgen, Roeselare, Diksmuide, Brugge, Middelkerke, ending back at Poperinge. In the evenings we'd mostly talk shop. I had to say something to Vito because I sensed he was becoming more apprehensive about the upcoming Tour.

"You can still cancel it all if you want," I told him honestly. "I don't think Corkscrew's money is actually in the hands of Contra-X. Vito, speak up. No great loss if you've changed your mind."

He sighed and began combing his hair and then smoothed his eyebrows with his palms. "No," he said slowly, "this will be my last chance. I feel it in my bones that I won't disgrace myself. After all, if I can't ride clear on the Izoard and simply stay in the bunch, who's to know of our little scheme? I'll withdraw and no-one will notice."

"I'm sorry," said Romain, "I'd like to let you break clear, but I can't do that, I have my own legend to maintain. So far my record's untainted. I'm out to win in France and Italy."

"You're a fool," I told him, "to ride the Giro d'Italia. Some have won the two Tours, but very few. I don't think you're going to be one of them. You know as well as I do there are more kudos attached to the Tour de France."

He didn't reply and went on eating his meal.

After a week we'd had enough of the Belgian circuit. Romain was due to compete, and Vito wanted to ride a minor, but hilly, event back in Italy.

"To test my legs," he said.

So what did I do? You guessed it.

"Can I speak to Germaine Sullavan if she's available."

We met in a quiet bar not far from the Stromboli. She looked stressed but I didn't put it like that. "You look a bit tired. Not sleeping well?"

"No, not at all well. It's this on-off movie thing. They keep holding damn meetings where no-one will agree on anything. You notice you're not invited. You who knows it like it was. I tell you, Terry, I can't see you getting a cent out of Metz. If they make the movie at all, they'll make it their way, and it'll be nothing like it really was. Suydam knocks every angle the others come up with. He gets paid so much that real money is like Monopoly money."

"Well it's true that the only real drama comes in the actual race. Before that it was just my bloody ordinary life."

She began playing with the strap on her handbag. "That's the bit they've got to hype up. Your ride as it happened can't be improved on although they'll try. They'll make you so 'interesting' that you won't recognize yourself. But I tell you—the movie won't be made. I feel it in my bones. Suydam'll get sidetracked by one of the many scripts that bounce off him. The man's a walking wanker, but his nod is final."

I didn't know what to say except a bland, "You're probably right."

She slid down an inch or two in her chair and closed her eyes. "What a world. I only hope for your sake that this Vito guy does his thing. Not that it makes sense to me. What is it really? A middle-aged Italian riding a bike uphill. Apologies to you, but I find grown men riding bicycles just a little comical. What's so special about this Vito thing? Does it prove anything?"

I had half a mind to let this bit of conversation die, to brush it aside with a laugh. But no, I bit.

"Oddly enough it does prove something. Not to you, not to anyone apart from Vito, Corkscrew, and myself. Even then, only if it comes off. We're playing a long shot, a very long one. Corkscrew isn't long for this world, he has the money and wants to see something 'magical' recaptured. And Vito? It's his last chance maybe to go out in a blaze of glory. Me? I'm the middle man."

"This Corkscrew guy must be loaded to pour money into something so weird when only three people'll get anything from it—however magical."

"Put like that, you're right. Sorry to hear you're feeling so low. Do you take sleeping pills?"

"Not if I can help it. Mostly I read till I'm cross-eyed."

"What are you reading?"

A smile spread across her face and she ran her tongue 'round the inside of her mouth. "It's a stunner. It's called *The Book of Marmalade and its Antecedents.*" She burst out laughing. "No, seriously, not that, but there actually was a book of that title. Do you read much?"

Not to be outdone, I fired back, "I can't put it down. It's called *Premature Burial and How it May be Prevented.*"

This amused her. A good moment, but I thought better of it and didn't kiss her. The gap stopped me, that gap between movie star and a nobody.

15. They'll Never Take Me Alive

Ryan and Cross began pressing me. They tried to get me to be official starter at some of the smaller events. In their minds a sort of exposure drive. I did a few and felt silly. Despite the fact that my Tour participation would be my swan song, I owed it to myself to do the best I could. A period of training began, done mostly on my own. The team itself had little time for training, as the events themselves began to stack up.

The movie project was in its death throes according to Germaine, and when it finally fizzled out she stayed on in France to do, she said, some sightseeing. We managed to meet, mostly in restaurants, and for a while I actually ding-donged between meetings with Germaine and Rosie, much to Throbbo's amusement. "What about the hard word?" he kept saying. "When's it gonna happen? You're like effing Peter Pan with a rose between yer teeth."

Never mind Throbbo. What I wanted was to get the Tour over with before thinking too hard about women. But it was not to be. Rosie wanted to see me, and there was an urgency in her voice, so we met at her hotel.

"I'm having to go home," she announced. "Margaret's done her thing and realized she'll always be an also-ran. It's costing an arm and a leg my staying on. But I can't leave without saying what's been on my mind for the past weeks."

"Okay." I pulled up a chair. "Let's hear it."

She walked up and down holding her chin. "I don't quite know how to put it. How to put it, that is, without sounding stupid and presumptuous." She fell silent but kept walking, then, "They say a woman can always tell. I only hope that's right. I sense in you, Terry, a feeling you have toward me. That sort of feeling if you know what I mean. What I want to say is, that although I can't afford to stay on in France, if you'd like to come to Australia when I've sorted my own problem out, you'd be very welcome."

She'd actually blushed and looked very embarrassed, so much so that I knew the time was right to hug and kiss her. But even with her in my arms I knew it wasn't right to push things further.

"Rosie, Rosie, of course I have feelings for you. Right now you're not free and I've got a barrel full of things coming up that I've got to get through. You go home, sort out your life, while I get on top of things here. These days you're only a few hours away. Let things settle. How does that sound? Don't let's get too involved right now in case things don't come out as hoped."

What I'd said to Rosie hadn't been planned, or even thought out. It was her speaking that did it, her honest and touching words that must have sparked off something in me I hadn't quite realized. I didn't want to regret it, but wanted to put it on hold for a while. And of course I still hankered after Germaine, even though I'd come to accept that she was suffering from quite a strong depression and was on medication. When I got around to mentioning the subject she was quite open about it.

"Sure I'm depressed. Who wouldn't be? Here I am clinging to the tail end of what I once was. I have no prospects for employment. I'm nearly broke. It seems the only solution is to go back to my husband, assuming he'll have me."

"Join me and everybody I know at life's crossroads," I said rather bitterly.

In spite of what had passed between me and Rosie, it was more curiosity than anything that made me blurt out, "How would you feel about coming in with me?"

"With you...?" she said slowly as if I'd spoken in a foreign tongue and she was mentally translating.

Retreating, I said, "Well, it's just a thought."

"Terry," she said breathlessly, "you're a nice guy. But your life—this Italian guy in the mountains and such things—isn't my life. I wouldn't say this to anyone else except you, but I've got to start coming to terms with the fact that life is rapidly passing me by. I regret my life. I've wasted it. If I'd known at the time what I know now... I read a poem once by Thomas Hardy. I forget what it was called, but these lines stuck. 'Childlike, I danced in a dream; Blessings emblazoned that day; Everything glowed with a gleam; Yet we were looking away.' That's been my life—looking away, not realizing what I had and wasting it. It sounds horrible, I know, but it would make a bit of difference if you were rich."

I felt sticky and awkward and wanted out of this one quickly. "Never mind. A few chapters from *Frog Raising for Pleasure and Profit* will put you right. Time I was leaving. I'll ring you next week."

* * *

At least with both women things were now out in the open and had moved up a notch. There were times when I felt I didn't want either, and moments later all would go into reverse. Anyway, I could probably count Germaine out—more's the pity. Yet I needed someone in my life, some stability, a home perhaps. All the things I would have had with Paula. Rosie was fine, and the more I thought about her the better she became. I'd had enough of this worrying void that came with Paula's death.

Then, just as things seemed to be running fairly smoothly, it happened. In my mind the movie title "Bad Day at Black Rock" wouldn't go away. There I was in bed when the phone rang which I naturally left to Throbbo to answer.

"Here," he said. "For you. Sounds like a foreigner."

It was Padovkin. "My apologies for this late hour."

Inwardly I groaned. It could only be about his damn bike. "I'm listening."

"Something very important has arisen. A fault has been detected within the frames. If I can return them to the manufacturer by tomorrow first thing, the fault will be rectified with no charge to me. But after tomorrow the cost will be mine. At considerable cost, unfortunately. I have three vehicles loaded, one each for Gloria and myself. Could you do me a great favor and drive the third, a Volvo station wagon?"

Before he'd finished I'd rapidly thought of several ways to say no. "What, at this hour? Can't it wait till tomorrow? And where are you going; not to Russia, surely?"

"No, no, not to Russia. Just into Germany. Today is the last day the repair clause operates, so I must be there first thing."

My conscience light came on, having taken the man's money where there was no hope of placing his cycle. "And there's no-one else you can ask? No-one at all?"

"Sadly, no."

He must have heard my big sigh. "Okay then."

The starting-out point was at the warehouse. When I arrived, there were three parked station-wagons. Moonless, it was pitch dark save for the cab lights on two of the vehicles. Padovkin was in one and Gloria's unmistakable white face peered anxiously from the other.

Padovkin came toward me. "Again my apologies," he began.

I was hunched, cold and disgruntled. "Never mind. Now what's the story? Do I simply follow you?"

"Of course. I will lead and Gloria will stay close behind me. You must keep with her because at one point I intend to take a short cut to save time."

I scanned the gloom and could see the three vehicles were stacked with bike frames.

"We shouldn't have to stop on the way. The vehicles are all topped up."

There didn't seem to be anything else to say. Not that I wanted to, I was that angry.

Once we got going, it dawned on me that if I lost contact, I hadn't a clue about the final destination. So I kept close to moon-faced Gloria. Traffic was beginning to thin out the further we went, but driving on someone else's stop lights isn't exactly relaxing.

We must have gone about fifty miles when I first became aware of a vehicle behind me. But I soon forgot it and lapsed back into anger and annoyance at Padovkin.

Around the hundred mile mark, it was still there. I assured myself that it was a main route and we'd probably got a similar destination.

And yet they were still there—a pair of headlights like unblinking eyes. I started to tell myself I'd seen too many cop movies. If I slowed down and forced the vehicle to overtake I would have lost contact with Gloria. I felt like meat in a sandwich, so on we went heading for the German border. At last I saw Gloria's indicator signalling a left turn. Now I'd shake my shadow off: I flicked my left indicator, catching my breath when the shadow turned with me.

My first thought was to jump Gloria and get ahead of her, so I got as close as I could. The road was a bit of a winder and I couldn't get enough straight to make the pass. Ahead of her, I could still see Padovkin's tail lights.

I'd only glanced away from my mirror for a few seconds, and there it was, right close to me. By now I was fully alerted, yet could do nothing. At last, seeing a straight length of road, I pulled out, only to slam my brakes on when my following shadow beat me to it and tore past, overtaking Gloria as well. I pulled as far as I could to the centre in time to see the shadow overtake Padovkin. At least I'd got rid of it, whatever it was, but could still do nothing except keep up with Gloria. We were all moving at a speed too fast for the road. A roadside sign showed more bends ahead.

I was gripping the wheel as if my life depended on it, and I flung the Volvo into bend after bend on Gloria's tail. Then it happened. Her stop lights came on and I stood on the brakes almost ramming her. Ahead, around the next bend, came the stab of headlights from what had to be Padovkin facing backward. Then in a tire-screaming reverse, Gloria backed past me catching my Volvo's wing. She stopped, tore open the door and beat on my vehicle's side. I half opened my door. She looked pale and wild, wide-eyed and trembling.

"Turn 'round! Go back!" she yelled and was gone, her frame-laden wagon disappearing back the way we'd come.

I didn't know what to do, what to think. As I slammed the door I heard what most definitely were two shots. That was enough for me. I did the fastest three-point turn on record, leaving tire marks all over the road as I pursued Gloria. For a few miles I did get glimpses of her tail lights until we got separated among heavy traffic and I lost contact. Once clear of the juggernauts, I put my foot down and headed back the way I'd come, arriving at Throbbo's in the early hours. I left the Volvo outside and crept back in, hoping not to disturb Throbbo and his wife.

But Throbbo, with his nose for trouble, was sipping a cognac, waiting.

"That was a night out you've just had." He pushed a coffee toward me and I gratefully took it.

"You can say that again. I've just relived The Big Sleep. Can Maria hear us?"

"No, she's asleep."

So I gave it to him just like it happened. He let out a low whistle and poured us both another coffee. "What d'you make of it? When you first told me about them I thought they sounded a couple of weirdos."

Chapter 15. They'll Never Take Me Alive

"I can't make anything of it. I've simply no idea. All I can do is sit tight, although when I've had a bit of a rest and something to eat, I'll dump the Volvo back at the warehouse and collect my car."

And that's what I did. I scrubbed my training schedule feeling that I should sit tight. But sit tight for what? Padovkin and Gloria could easily find out where I was living via my phone number. I hoped they would show up and explain everything.

By the following day, I'd got fed up sitting around and did a quick fifty kilometers on my cycle. When I got back, Throbbo took me to one side. He was holding a folded newspaper. "Listen to this. It's only a short bit." He looked around to make sure he wasn't overheard: "Nancy. Police are investigating a shooting which took place on the night of the twenty-fifth. The body of Michael Padovkin was found in the seat of a station-wagon containing cycle frames. Death was from gunshot wounds. Police are continuing with their enquiries."

Although I scanned all the newspapers and heard just about every news item, there was nothing further. That is until Gloria suddenly appeared. Throbbo's café was busy. She said nothing but stood there next to a small Citroën, waiting for me to speak. I took her elbow and led her away from the café.

"I guess you've got a few things to tell me," I said sharply.

She shuddered like a huge jelly. "Poor Michael is dead, shot." "I'd sort of gathered that. I was there, don't forget. What's it all about, Gloria? Who shot Michael and why? What gives?"

"Can we sit quietly somewhere?"

I led her across the square to a public seat.

"I'm leaving," she began, something I'd already gathered on seeing the piled suitcases on the back seat of her car.

She placed one of her large white hands on my knee in a token of confidentiality. "I'll tell you the truth, Mr. Davenport. Michael used your current profile as a front. He knew, and I expect you knew, there would be no Tour de France interest in his cycle. It was a brilliant invention as a utility cycle, that's all. This before he got entwined in drugs. There are certain men—I will not name them—in Russia who saw the potential for getting cocaine and other banned drugs into France and beyond. The fat tubing on the frames was ideal." She groped inside her handbag and pulled out what looked like an oversize condom. "In these. As the frames were easily dismountable it was simple. Michael knew you had no chance placing the racing frames and he bought you to give himself a front, to show your picture at the customs and to any enquiring officialdom. He reasoned your recent profile would be reasonably well known. We Russians are always suspect. Initially Michael was within the law, but was pulled into the drug business where, if he didn't play ball, his family was threatened. But he got greedy and kept the proceeds of one shipment to himself."

I'd often thought Kafka had had a hand in scripting my life: I could hardly believe what I was hearing. "And that's why he was killed?"

"Michael was a good honest man until he came under the power of criminals. His bicycle was his whole life."

"So I was a patsy, the face of respectability."

"The borders are now almost wide open, but you never know. He carried this large photo of you to show enquirers, you, our agent in France, the famous Tour rider."

"Do any of these gangsters know about me? They might wonder if Michael had told me any of their tie-ups and dropped a few names."

"I'm sure you are safe. He wouldn't have told you, the person he was using. But I know too much, that's why I'm going home to Georgia. There's nothing written. All his dealings were done verbally."

"Like Hitler," I commented. "Although they tailed me there was no way I could warn Michael. Could they trace me through the Volvo's number plate?"

"I think not. All three vehicles were hired under his name. Those men had given him a deadline, which had just passed, for returning the money he'd kept for himself. Initially Michael didn't believe they'd harm his family, but as the deadline passed he got scared and panicked. The frames had to go back—there were never more than forty—for refilling."

"Taking the empties back," I said dryly.

"Fortunately Michael kept my name out of all these dealings and gave me the name of Gloria."

"As we're finally being honest, were you his mistress?"

"Oh, yes, oh, yes."

"Okay Gloria, best you beat it. Sadly I can't. I suppose my Volvo's still outside the warehouse?"

"I believe so. They have been hired for two weeks."

I waved the fat lady goodbye and went back to the warehouse armed with surgical spirit and rags, all to wipe my finger prints off the vehicle.

It was a wonder it hadn't been stolen, the damaged wing probably putting thieves off. My intention was to wipe it clean and leave it there. I did it thoroughly—steering wheel, gear change, handbrake, indicators. It was while doing the gear lever that my pen fell out of my top pocket and disappeared down the side of the seat. That I had to retrieve; my prints were all over it. Try as I did I couldn't reach it. I took a big screwdriver from my tool kit and used it to gently lever the seat clear of its fixing.

Under the seat was a wrapped parcel. My first thoughts were that it probably contained more drugs and was best left alone. Curiosity won and I opened it. At first I thought they must be counterfeit. I couldn't believe my eyes. There were neatly tied bundles of notes in a mix of currencies. And there were a lot of them, enough to send the old heartbeats up a few revs.

Panicking a little, I did a quick last minute wipe and got out quick, my mind racing all the way back to Throbbo's. I coaxed him into a shed at the bottom of the property.

"Here, take a look at this little lot. Hidden under the Volvo's front seat."

It takes a lot to get Throbbo excited, and now was one of those rare times.

"Jesus Christ! Look at them! Are they real? Swiss francs, English pounds, lire, deutschmarks!"

"I wonder what it all amounts to?"

"God knows. I'd have to get the exchange rates from the bank. They're still open. I'll nip out now."

We hid the money and I waited. A couple of times I found myself checking my pulse.

"Not a word to Maria," he said when he returned. "She'd want to hand it over to the police. And I can't see you doing that."

Between serving in the café, Throbbo spent the rest of the day punching a calculator.

Had Padovkin intended to pay back what he'd creamed off for himself and got shot before he could explain? Clearly Gloria didn't know about it. Maybe Padovkin had it earmarked to give to his family. Probably I'd never know. But with a few taps on Throbbo's calculator, I'd suddenly become quite well-heeled despite giving half to Throbbo. A quick working out made it come to about a hundred thousand dollars each.

But was I safe? Were the bad guys looking for me? Not wanting to bring trouble onto Throbbo, I immediately took a one-bedroom flat close by. Nice to be able to afford it.

"If some hoods come here looking for me, tell them the truth; don't bring yourself any bother. I can take care of myself."

"I suppose you could return the money if your life depended on it," Throbbo said without much conviction.

"This cash has saved me, do you realize that? I won't give it up easily."

"You remind me of the Jack Benny joke where he was held up. 'Your money or your life! Why don't you answer?' 'I'm thinking about it.' Have you still got your bang-bang?"

"Not handy. It's in a safe deposit box."

He reached up to a rafter on the shed roof and pulled down a plastic wrap. "It ain't much. Just a wobbly .32 H&R. But just having it could change events."

I stuck the revolver in my hip pocket. Watching me, Throbbo gave me a gentle shove. "Like the old days, eh?"

As I nodded agreement, a few flashes from the past popped up.

"Except we only carried them for bravado. This one might be the real thing."

16. Pennies From Heaven

Days went by and between us we unloaded the notes, either at banks or exchange bureaux. I opened another bank account and deposited my share. I'd barely got over all that excitement when Throbbo called in to say a hospital had rung to say that Ronald Parker—Corkscrew—was ensconced there and would I phone them.

I straight away went over to Throbbo's and rang the number they'd given.

"Corkscrew, it's me. What are you doing in hospital?"

"Ah, Terry-lad. I'm so glad you've called. No, what's happened is that I've had a turn for the worse. I booked myself in here. It's a private hospital, and they're supposed to be among the best."

Although I'd guessed what the trouble was, I had to ask, "Why, what's wrong?"

"I told you they'd sliced a bit off the old prostate because it was cancerous. Well, it's opened the floodgates and it's spread."

"Bloody hell. Can they do anything?"

"Afraid not. Oh, they say they can but that's just talk to make me comfortable. No, mate, I've had it."

"Don't say that. There must be hope, surely?"

"Nope. Anyway, I thought I'd bring you up to date. Contra-X have been paid. I've already got a huge TV set installed in my room so, please God, I can see what Vito does. That's all there is for me now. I hope to God he doesn't disappoint me. He's still okay, isn't he?"

"Sure, sure. We stay in touch. Contra-X had to upset things to justify his inclusion. Some of your money probably had to go to their weakest rider to sort of buy him off, to pacify his being dropped."

"Yes, that would have upset the apple cart. So it's all on course?" He was beginning to sound very distant, so I wound up my call.

"At the moment, yes. I've had a bit of financial luck but I'll tell you next time. Is there anything you need?"

"No, they can't do enough for me. Can you pop in again? Funny old world, innit?"

"Sure. Now take it easy."

Corkscrew's image filled my thoughts. The end of a man up there in a little room. And me? First the whole bloody Padovkin business, which as far as I knew might not be over. Then, on the face of it, instant wealth. And now poor Corkscrew. Life goes up and life goes down.

Chapter 16. Pennies From Heaven

A short while later I visited him. He didn't have to tell me again there was no hope: it was written all over his face.

"We're alike, you and me" he said. "A couple of also-rans who pounded the route most of our lives with not much to show for it. Then I had the big Lotto win. Now you've netted yourself a little pile. To get our riches, neither of us did very little. Yet the world's awash with money, and women too, but I could never get either through effort. Cash and crumpet—they were everywhere, but not for me and probably not for you."

I knew that if I didn't ask him then I might not get another chance.' "How did you get the name Corkscrew?"

"My name? Not what some people might think. It's because I've always had a cock-eyed way of looking at things. Leastways I always stood out as being different, you know —bent. Funny old world," he said and fell asleep.

* * *

The Giro d'Italia loomed, and there was much activity among the teams. Boretti, who was in charge of our team, hadn't much time to talk to anyone, and I was out on a limb of my own making. I tut-tutted at Romain's participation but said no more. Anyway, it was in his contract to take part, being a star rider.

My flat had turned out to be a disaster, and I got my stuff together ready to return to Throbbo's until the Tour was over. After that I wasn't sure what to do because there now seemed many possibilities. The flat wasn't conducive to sound sleep, which I needed. The whole apartment block was lit up at night like the last hours of the Titanic and the noise on a par with Soviet tanks entering Prague.

It was my last night there when a knock came on the door followed by the bell being pressed. Only Throbbo knew I was there, and that approach was definitely not his.

I unzipped one of my packed bags and took out Throbbo's ·32. Standing clear of the door I said, "Who's there?"

"Open and you'll find out."

A woman's voice, but it was faint and I couldn't place it. I stuck the revolver in my waistband and opened the door.

"Found you," Susan said. "Throbbo told me where you were hiding."

Yes, I was stunned and probably showed it. "Susan," I said stupidly. "Where the hell have you been?"

"Out and around. I gather you've been looking for me?"

"I have and you know why."

"Oh. The money. You'd like it back."

"Well, it is mine. And you've come to give it back?"

"Can I come in?"

"Sure." I stood aside and looked her up and down. She wasn't a very attractive woman. Tall, slim and somewhat gawky, she had a thin featureless face, on this occasion well made up. She wore an expensive black suit and a white blouse held at the neck by some sort of cravat. Swinging a small black handbag she turned to face me.

"How's life?"

"What do you want, Susan?"

"We had our moments, didn't we?" She took a few paces 'round the room, still swinging the handbag. Then she stopped and looked directly at me.

"I put it to you, Terry, like this. Since I last saw you, I've been around more than somewhat. Know what? There are a lot of men out there. I guess I've had a fair sampling. But you know—they were all wankers. Each and every one. Attractive? Sure, but that's all. You once told me I was a top screw—as you so romantically put it. On reflection, I see you now as, well, not a bad bloke. What I'm suggesting is that we forget the past and get together. We got on fine, didn't we?"

She watched me ease the revolver from my waistband, unzip the holdall and put it back in.

"Expecting trouble?" She sounded a bit scared.

"No, just returning it to Throbbo. Let's be mercenary for a moment. By that I mean money."

She sat down, crossed her legs, and took a check book from her bag. "It was roughly ten thousand pounds, wasn't it? Not much to show for a life of pedaling. Make it out to cash, shall I?"

"Hang on," I told her and sat opposite. "You know, I could never trust you. You play the game the whole time.

Me today, someone else tomorrow. To be honest I never cared much for you. Lustful moments when Paula was out, quickies in the back of my car. A sort of adventure for both of us. Top screw? I may have said it, but you aren't. No, Susan, keep the bloody money. You intended to anyway, and I could never trust you. I've had a bit of luck and don't need the likes of you now."

She opened the check book and signed it, tore the check out and put the book back in her bag. Her smile was the sort you hook over your ears with effort.

"This must be a unique moment in your life, Terry, turning down money and a screw. That must have been a lot of luck you've had."

"Money helps," I said, "it sure helps."

She edged toward the door. I opened it and she stood there. After searching my face, she said, throwing the check on the floor, "You fill in the details. I made a mistake, you're a wanker like the rest of 'em."

Swinging her handbag, she marched off and I closed the door, not only on her but all that had gone before.

＊　＊　＊

Once back at Throbbo's, a period of intense activity grabbed me. The Tour was getting uncomfortably close, and I was having thoughts, most of them second thoughts, about it.

Chapter 16. Pennies From Heaven

I wanted to give Romain some support during the Tour of Italy, but I simply couldn't spare the time. He'd clinched the King of the Mountains title, but only just, making the mistake of holding back on the big climbs and trying to take the primes and time bonuses over the last few hundred yards. At this he was beaten a few times by an up-and-coming Spanish climber. I'd told him enough times that his strength was in attacking early and turning on the power. There were no current climbers who could withstand this remorseless wearing down that Romain was so good at. He did a devastating ride on the Cuneo–Pinerolo stage that dramatically sealed his Mountain title. For all that, he only managed fourth place overall.

I reached him by phone the day after the race finished. He sounded withdrawn and reluctant to speak.

"What's up? You did well. Next year you'll get it. See, you should have stuck with the advertising lady."

"I suppose fourth isn't too bad. The finishes were so hard fought. Every other rider is a sprinter. I couldn't get a look in. Terry, there's something I ought to tell you. I'm not sure even if I should."

"Go on, then. I'm over twenty-one."

"Don't get mad, will you? Well, you might. Well, you should. Don't say I told you, promise?"

"Okay, okay, spill it."

"I overheard a conversation between Cross and Ryan. They were talking about you. Cross said that you'd probably end in the gutter like you did in last year's Tour. Because the gutter was where you belonged. What a sod of a thing to say."

For a long moment I didn't answer while mentally my fist landed on Cross's face. I didn't want to show Romain how those words affected me, and I brushed them aside as best I could. "Ah, well, you know what a nasty piece of work he is. It's the sort of thing you'd expect from him. Better forget it. All you've got to do now is think about the Tour de France. Me too."

17. May the Gods Preserve

I didn't know it at the time, but when I met Germaine in a bar after a fairly long time gap, that it would be the last time I saw her. A steely line or two had crept in around the corners of her mouth.

"Hi," she said with a sigh, and sat opposite me. "They've all gone—Metz, Suydam, the whole damn lot. Lucky I've got an open ticket, so I've hung on to let them get clear."

As I had to put in a good afternoon's work behind the motor pacer, I couldn't stay long. She sensed my urgency.

"Not keeping you, am I?" There was a tinge of bitterness in her voice which the smile failed to conceal.

I tried to relax. "No, not at all. It's great to see you again. You're set on going home, are you?"

She nodded from behind a cloud of cigarette smoke. "Sure. Where else?"

"The us-together theme still doesn't interest you?" Because I'd raised the question, I felt I should ask her this.

"I guess not, Terry. It has its attractions, but long-term I wouldn't know where we were going."

"Not even if I've come into some worthwhile money?"

She didn't answer.

"Several hundred grand," I lied.

A bemused smile. "Terry, Terry. The husband I guess I'll return to would put a figure like that down to expenses. I don't want to sound cruel, but it's peanuts, and as far as the you-me situation goes, money doesn't much come into it. No, I've got to do something with my life, wave goodbye to tinsel-town, find a purpose. But the sad bit is that whatever I do, there'll come a time when someone's going to say, 'Do you remember that old biddy: she used to be in movies'. And that time draws near, day after every fucking day."

After we'd had a couple of drinks, I watched her walk away.

"'Bye, Terry, good luck with the Tour de France, for you and the old Italian riding uphill. Give us a ring, I'm still at the Stromboli."

Such is life that you can never know when anything's for the last time.

＊　＊　＊

Chapter 17. May the Gods Preserve

The Tour de France was too close for me to dwell on Susan's surprise visit. True, it spoilt a couple of night's sleep, even though I knew it was something I had to snap out of. While the Tour of Italy was finishing, I'd arranged for a pacer sometimes used by Boretti to scooter-pace me over the course of the Tour de France's first stage. This 174 kilometers between Metz (not him again!) and Reims were best done in the early hours.

As long as a rider is up to it, he can go a lot faster being paced. Prolonged speed was what I was aiming for, the hoped-for ability to hold it, fast, hour after hour, yet still retain something, to thrash it, turn on the power, never give up. Dreaming again, Terry Davenport, whom may the gods preserve.

The pacing went well, and I could pound the highest gear all right, a gear higher than I'd normally use in a road race. I'd got to know that road pretty well over the two weeks before the Giro ended, and it was then that I had a chance to talk with Boretti and the team. Cross's snide remark about me ending in the gutter had cemented my determination to do more than show the advertisers' colors. A smouldering determination to actually take the first stage had taken root inside me.

I treated the team to a swell meal and get-together in a private suite. I couldn't help myself: I chose the Stromboli. I guess she was out someplace—just as well because I was probably trying to impress her.

Before the party broke up, I tried again to ring Cork-screw. That was the third attempt and been told he was asleep. My suspicion was that he was under sedation. The worry that was beginning to crowd in had a picture of him not being conscious when and if Vito accomplished something. Yet if Vito failed and was simply dropped, perhaps it was just as well if Corkscrew missed it. The closer the event came, the more I could see it all falling apart.

I let them all eat and drink first and air all the anecdotes about the Tour of Italy. I stood up and tapped my wine glass with a spoon like they all do at meetings in the movies.

"Okay, fellas, I need to run through it all again about the Tour, and in particular the first stage. For personal reasons, which I doubt any of you would understand, I hope, really hope, to win it. Now I know what you're thinking, and probably you're right. Just the same I want to try. And to do it, I need the help of each and every one of you. No point my telling you it's a cow of a stage unless you happen to be a top sprinter who'd aim to take victory on the finishing line. So, what to do? Last year I sort of fixed a win for a young Australian girl who was over here. It was nothing clever and as old as the hills, and you'll all know it. Yet it still appears to work. It's this: for a rider or riders to go right at the start and gain a lead. The bunch, and certainly the star riders, won't bother at that point. Perhaps any riders who might live in that area will want to show off. Who knows? We'll only know on the day.

Chapter 17. May the Gods Preserve

"You'll be aware already of what I'm going to say. Get as many of our lot as possible out there, out in front, leaving some to follow up and try to slow any pursuers. I'd have to take off and try to catch the initial breakaways. Once caught, they pace me. With luck, a couple of you should be coming up fast to relieve the first break, afterward combining to keep me out in front.

"Now we all know it almost certainly won't happen quite like that. Some dangerous sprinters may tag along. Maybe that first break will be pulled back before anyone can do anything. The worst scenario is that it all works and the bunch swamps me close to the finish, assuming I'd even get that far.

"What I've been doing is going over the course, scooter paced, hoping—and this is my only hope—that I can just scrape home before the mob overhauls me. Near the end I'd have to come up with that mixture of long sprint and short break, neither one thing nor the other. If I can do anything, not being a climber or a sprinter, is turn in a sustained solo. Can I do it? Will it work? I need you guys, all of you, to get me clear and keep me there. Can I count on you?"

The responses came—Oui, si, sure, of course, naturellement.

One of them, Lando, began thumping the table and raised his glass at me followed by the others.

Then Boretti got to his feet. "There, Terry, that's support for you. No rider could ask for more."

151

I felt good. "No, that's great. And it goes without saying that if the plan falls apart, any of you who are well placed, forget me and go for it."

18. I Shall Return

Metz. The hype that was in full swing seemed worse than in previous years. In some ways I can accept it; after all it's been going since 1903, and I'm all in favor of holding on to tradition, the past, in a world spiralling into god-knows-what.

They made quite a thing of Vito and me—the two old 'uns. The underlying implication was that we were something of a joke, more to be pitied for thinking we had a chance. I suspect the minds of many visualized the pair of us hopelessly burnt off, dismounting, legs like rubber, helped by men in white coats into a waiting vehicle.

I still felt good about myself despite lingering apprehension about the Padovkin business. No arrests had been made and there had been nothing further in the press for quite a while. I was assuming with fingers crossed that no-one could link me to the affair.

"I'll be glad when it starts," Vito said under his breath, as cameras clicked and we held our smiles. "I'll play it like we agreed."

"That's all you can do," I concurred, "just as long as you can stay in the race no matter how lowly placed you are. I wonder what they'd say if they knew we were both here for one stage apiece."

"But I'll have to do more than play it solo," he said, running his hand along the saddle of his machine. "I'll have to do what I can as a team rider. I only hope that doesn't take too much out of me. I'll be looking for the easiest ride possible down to the Alps."

"How do you feel, Vito? All this for the last time."

"I feel kind of sad. For all the hardships, it's been my life, and I still can't see anything beyond it. I'm not looking forward to retirement. What will I do? Chase more women? Fuck myself into the ground? Somehow even that has lost some of its appeal. It's all bullshit, really, isn't it? It's commerce, you know, Terry, commerce. Getting the best you can with what you've got to offer. Possessing or being possessed by the best deal you can get. And what about you, Terry, what now?"

It was about thirty minutes before the start, and my adrenalin was doing a quickstep. "Like you, I guess. I can't imagine life without all this. We'll know soon enough."

I'd told Vito the Padovkin story. He shrugged and gave that sly little smile of his. "If nothing else, it's changed your life: couldn't have happened to a nicer guy."

So there I was rolling forward at the start, one of the two oldest men in the race. I managed a short wave to Vito, but he soon became lost among the mass of riders. The fanfares, the music, the TV cameras all bounced off me. The beginning of the end of my world. What was left of it was ahead on the road to Reims.

Not long after the neutralized section and the race had left the city outskirts, the pace got into its stride.

The weather was good for my hoped-for plan. A head wind would have made it almost impossible—like pushing sand uphill, but unless it changed, it was to one side and blowing slightly from behind.

We'd spent hours going over exactly what to expect. Pozzo was our best climber, so I wanted him to take off first. All the riders would know a climber breaking straight away on the first, flat stage wouldn't lead to anything. Next to go would be Lando, a strong experienced man, soon followed by Colombat who should link with Lando. These two and Pozzo would be my pacers, I hoped. With so many fresh young pros, how many would go along with a break hoping to make their mark?

Somewhere along the route I'd be the next to go and try making contact with the three team men ahead. Once I'd got clear, Zanoni and Costa were the final breakaways coming up from behind. The remaining four team men back in the bunch were to do what they could to hinder any pursuers.

Now this may have sounded fine, but the other hundred and seventy professionals were there to win too. I made sure I held a place close to the rest of the team and to Pozzo in particular.

He went almost straight away to loud cheers from the lines of pressing spectators, his audacity drawing laughter mixed with the shouts of encouragement. Go, Pozzo, go I hummed to myself. Several riders thought they'd catch some of the limelight as well, but soon eased back into the bunch.

Pozzo was now the center of TV attention. One of the Tour's helicopters cast a shadow across the road as it filmed Pozzo's big solo effort.

I could see him ahead, probably holding about forty-four kilometers an hour to the bunch's forty. I felt that riders weren't going to waste energy so very early in the race and were content to wait nearer the finish before getting aggressive.

He had a lead of a couple of hundred yards before Lando and Colombat went, Lando first, then Colombat minutes later.

There were glances going on all around me. Three riders clear—were they going to let them go, wear themselves out and take them later? Or would they pull them back for being so cheeky? These were the silent thoughts that buzzed back and forth. I waited to see what they were going to do. In the middle of a fast moving bunch, riders inches apart travelling at times close to forty kilometers an hour, there's never a lot of opportunity for discussion. One moment of inattention can sometimes cause a terrible crash.

No, the leading riders didn't seem put out by what was happening. I reckon the general thought was that Lando was being set up for a win. If that had been the case, it would have been a long hard haul for any rider.

It was too early for me to break. Once out there on my own, there was no going back. I steamed along fast, elbow to elbow, keep up, keep close to the wheel in front, mind the riders on each side, watch the road.

Beneath all the concentration a second layer of thought wouldn't go away. A nagging question that wouldn't stop—has this Thing I once had, this prime of life—whatever it was, had it left me? Was it the last embers of youth, a fading spark? Despite assuring medical tests, this Thing slides away. Does it go in the night like a ghost, or is it like a slowly dripping tap? Or like a disappointed lover creeping quietly away in the small hours? Every older rider must have been aware of it, however faintly.

Forty kilometers to go. There were a few short minor breaks, all soon absorbed by the steamrolling bunch. Still out front were my three with the same hundred yard advantage. I nursed the hope and clung to it that the trio wouldn't run out of steam. They'd been in camera most of the day collecting their share of glory, warriors of the road making their mark on the first day.

I had to go soon. If the trio cracked and I was on my own, I'd be sucked back as if caught in a huge vacuum cleaner. I remember clearly glancing up at the blue sky. There was no revelation, no giant finger pointing from the heavens, no stirring music. Just the roar and the clapping from the crowd and the whole damn noise of vehicles, bicycles, voices. How appropriate all that hubbub was. And there I was, steeling myself for the moment I'd planned, trained for and dreamt of. The big moment in my life? Maybe. What would Germaine say? A middle-aged man riding a bike along a road in France. At that moment I felt it was my whole life and I'd be judged by what I was about to attempt, even if nobody but myself cared. All the money I now had didn't seem to matter, not on that day. Nothing mattered except that line across the road at Reims.

I edged closer to Zanoni and Costa. They saw me and knew the moment had come. I hedge-hopped one rider at a time until I found myself next to the leaders. No-one took any notice. Ahead the straight, straight road. Nothing for it but to go. A slightly higher gear, a big lungful of air, head down, go.

For several minutes I dare not look back. I'd really thrashed the gear and had opened a twenty-five yard gap. The pack, spread out across the road, appeared unmoved, leaving an impression of row after row of impervious faces. I couldn't detect any great panic. All I had to do was thrash it, thrash it, open that gap.

Colombat began to ease, leaving Lando and Pozzo to hold the pace out front until Colombat and I connected. The man glistened with sweat but managed a quick grin as I fell into position behind him. Gradually he paced me up to the others.

And that was how we held it, mile after mile, Colombat, Lando and Pozzo taking turns at the front, each giving his utmost before slipping back while another did his share.

We still held about a two hundred yard lead. What had happened behind wasn't so good. Zanoni and Costa had got clear but had three other riders in tow. I couldn't make out who they were. If they were sprinters, then our two men dare not bring them close and had to do the reverse by slowing down even if it meant rejoining the bunch. A powerful sprinter sitting on my tail was the last thing I needed.

But they were playing it right, keeping between us and the main group, there in case needed. As Pozzo and Lando switched positions, Pozzo gulped 'Romain' at me so that I quickly threw a rearward peep. Sure enough, one of the pursuers was Romain. This I was not happy about. Romain, being a hot favorite to win the Tour, wouldn't have been allowed to gain any time, however slight, before the mountains. His presence stirred a reaction from the main group and so a big effort to rein in the breakaways began. And in a matter of minutes the escapees behind us were absorbed.

Immediately the tough Costa hit back, opening another lead but taking Romain clear. This time there was less response, and I guessed why. Coming up was the 10 km sign showing we were entering the last stretch of the stage. Romain couldn't gain any dangerous time in so short a distance, and already the big sprinters were edging toward the front.

My team mates were nearly shot. They all had expressions I'm more than familiar with. There wasn't much fight left in any of them, each one a great rider, each one on that day better than me. But still they switched and changed positions to shelter me.

Down that interminable straight road the four of us powered. Team vehicles behind were holding back, leaving their riders clear for the coming mass finish. Glimpses of buildings caught my eye: we had to be near, very near as we shot 'round a traffic island. Three kilometers to go and still, magically, a two-hundred yard lead, although I sensed a couple of riders clear ahead of the bunch and somewhere not too far behind me if I'd dared to look.

First Lando went, shaking his head as if to say sorry and soon Pozzo followed him. Colombat, gritting his teeth, did all he could but fell back and I easily overtook him.

I forged on alone toward the open mouth of a short tunnel. Had I still got enough punch in my legs? All (ha!) I had to do was pound those cranks 'round and 'round until they talked to me, to give it everything until it hurt and everything that was in me screamed.

Out of the tunnel and a turn to the right—POW! My God! It happened! I knew all right what it was. I could scarce believe it—a puncture! The rear tire was as flat as afternoon Swiss TV. I braked to a standstill. Where the hell were Lando and Colombat?

Lando? Lando? No! Out from the shadow of the tunnel came Romain. He was going to take the stage. Take if from me. Nothing could stop him. I'd lost, lost within spitting distance of the finish. I was about to fling my bike at him or any rider who came past. Yet he stopped, jumped off and thrust his machine at me.

"Get on!" he gasped. "They'll never catch you now. You're forgiven."

It felt like I was caught in a speeded up Charlie Chaplin film. I was on his machine and away, go-go-go, not even thinking about what he'd said, not till much later that day.

The puncture had lost me many seconds. Clear, vividly clear, fanned out across the boulevard came the bunch powering along fifty yards behind me, sprinters judging their efforts, jostling for positions, my shattered trio still trying and failing to slow the oncoming onslaught.

In moments I'd found the gear I wanted. This was it. I gave it everything, maybe everything I'd ever had plus a bit more. I could hear them close behind me, coming on fast, so fast, gaining on me by leaps and bounds. I felt half blind from the effort—was it tears, me, tears? Couldn't be, not me. I remember the blurred road stretching ahead, illusory, like a grey winding defile to nowhere. Hazy visions dance before me. Rosie touching my arm and saying "Oh, Terry, Oh, Terry." The look on Germaine's beautiful face as she shook her head in despair at me but still smiling. And Paula out there someplace wondering what our lives would have been like. A cavalcade of pictures? No, flashes, like bolts of lightning. Behind, that ominous whirr of a hundred machines bearing down, louder, closer, the cries of the crowds battering your brain, willing you to be caught or to hold out, to just make it to the line, or to collapse.

This strange feeling kept rising inside me. No, it wasn't extra energy or a new strength. It came like a stab of certainty that I would win. I felt it welling up: it was a thing I couldn't, nor wanted, to stop. I knew I had to do this thing for the friends who were watching, and those who weren't. I suppose, looking back, that I drew a sort of power from them. From Corkscrew, and Vito and Germaine and Rosie and Margaret and Paula and Throbbo. I couldn't fail them or myself, me who was nothing and was doing something, something... not ending in the dirt. This rising surge coming up from my knotted gut took on Germaine's voice and rattled through me like a stick on railings. "You're a loser, like me." And although she was right, today I'd prove her wrong. I knew it like I'd never known anything. My speed seemed unbelievable even though it couldn't have been and was a crazy hallucination. That big gear I'd felt too high to use was fairly spinning, talking to me, not seeming high enough. Everything ahead was a haze of moistening vision, not of sorrow, but certainty.

And so it was. It was all over. Officials were waving me down but I couldn't stop. The last meter, the last meter ever. That funny haze began to clear when I realized people were scattering before me. Hands on brakes, pull hard, slowly to a standstill. Joy and congratulations, back slapping, cold sponge—then suddenly a great weakness, but I couldn't dismount like some stiff old man. I gathered some dregs of strength and got off the bike with a casual sweep as somebody caught it.

The last meter, and I'd done it by a mere twenty. Once more, and for a few hours only because now I really had quit, a yellow jersey.

19. The Hammer Comes Down

At last. At last I could stretch out on a hotel bed. The place was bursting at the seams, chock full of Tour people. On the foot of the bed was the yellow jersey, the final one to my modest collection from last year.

I sensed Vito on the next bed keep glancing at me. Quietly he said, "That's your bit done. You know, I really thought they'd catch you. I was way back and couldn't see anything, but from snatches of radio commentary I thought you were done for."

"It was close," I sighed. "Thank God I haven't got to defend the jersey tomorrow. I'll turn down what food that's coming and tell 'em I don't feel too good. By morning I'll be real groggy and not start. It'll make a few headlines, but soon forgotten. What's waiting for you is a lot harder than what I've done."

Stretching and rubbing his temples, he said slowly, "I'm afraid you're right."

I closed my eyes and relived it all again. Dearly I'd have liked a go at Cross, but if I did he'd know Romain had passed on the overheard remark. I didn't need any of them now just as long as nothing nasty via Padovkin came up. I felt I was free. And even if it was my last ride, it was also my best. Although I couldn't have done it without the sacrifice made by the team. I'd acknowledged the plaudits, stood smiling on the rostrum, been photographed a hundred times, signed autographs, spoken into microphones, and now it was all over. Rosie and Margaret had been there with big hugs, but I was shipped away calling over my shoulder "I'll contact you tomorrow." And then, for the first time, I got a strong whiff of Romain and Margaret being more than nodding acquaintances. And what did he mean saying I was forgiven? It could only mean he knew about Susan and myself. This thought sent a stab of guilt through me, and I resolved to ignore what he'd said in case I was guessing right.

Later a grave looking Romain came in to shake my hand. He waved my thanks aside. "You've helped me on the route more times than I can repay. You were great today. You've still got it."

Doing what he'd done for me had pushed his position down, but not by much, the service vehicle and a rapid wheel change were soon on the scene. At that stage of the race the finishing times between first and last were sometimes mere seconds. A climber like Romain could easily make this up in the mountains.

It had been a busy time for Throbbo, and he couldn't get away. Later, when Romain had gone, I rang him. "You old sod. You pulled it off. I must admit I had many doubts. So now it's all over and you went out with a bang. No-one noticed me when I quit."

Next I wanted to phone Germaine. I'd told her the times to be watching on TV, but I couldn't get near a phone. I hated all these new-fangled things but by nine o'clock that evening I asked Romain if I could use his mobile.

"I knew it would be you," she said. "Congratulations. My hero! How do you feel?"

"Recovered, just about. For me it was quite a thing. Daft as it may sound, I discovered for the second time something inexplicable about myself. But never mind, I'm finished with it all now, bar seeing Vito's hoped-for ride. I've been wondering, are you going back to your marriage?"

I could tell by the long pause that she was surprised. "Oh! A leading question. I don't know. Probably. Sex is the game, marriage the penalty. You know, I'm tired of counting the dollars and frankly I'm tired of men in general even though you are a sweetie. They're all at it—old men, half-wits, actors, politicians, the lot. All fondling their danglers in the hope of sticking them somewhere." She gave a short laugh, and I said, "It's a great game, isn't it? Thank God I'm impotent and due for the priesthood."

A longer laugh. "Yes, I bet."

It all went much as I'd planned. Concerned faces peered into mine as the doctor announced that he couldn't find anything wrong with me. As I'd hardly eaten, they couldn't come up with the sabotage theory. No, it was a stomach upset and up to me whether I started the stage. Luckily Ryan, who knew all about it, was there to bustle the crowd out and close the door. To make it look good, I stayed in bed most of the day and managed a furtive bite when no-one was looking. The evening sports pages were full of my mystery illness, all of which made me cringe somewhat.

In the afternoon I managed to contact Corkscrew. He sounded very tired and didn't want to talk much and kept saying, "You're a good lad, a good lad. A great ride, really great."

The orderly attending Corkscrew mercifully spoke quite good English, and I managed to get his assurance that Corkscrew's TV would be on when the big mountain stage was shown. I had to trust the man. He did say off his own bat that he'd do his best within reason to keep the sedation down at the crucial time.

I gave it a couple of days before resurfacing, and when I did, it was to join Boretti in the team vehicle. Besides, I wanted to keep an eye on Romain as well as on Vito.

One by one I ticked off the fast, flat stages, each one being fought out by sprinters chasing the green jersey awarded for points gained on the finishing line—Dunkerque, Treport, Caen, St Brieuc, Brest, Quimper, St Nazaire, Royan, Bordeaux, Dax.

There's a saying that the Tour doesn't start until it reaches the mountains: for me this has always been true. Romain held on to his seventh position overall, while Vito stayed well down at the tail of the field. He'd simply kept at the rear of the main peloton, unnoticed by everyone although one newspaper did a cartoon suggesting he was out for a new record by finishing last.

Boretti had his suspicions about Vito's presence. Why would Corkscrew pour in cash just so Vito could creep along near last? He never said anything to me, but I think he sensed something of the plot.

I'd got a few brief calls through to Corkscrew, drawing a blank when he was sedated. Once though I got him when he was quite lucid.

"He'll do it, won't he? Tell him I said that. I think about him all the time. If he can pull it off, it'll be something, something great, something not of this horrible age, proof there are still a few worthwhile heroic things left."

This was good, because I think Vito also saw it in this inexplicable light. He nodded when I delivered Corkscrew's message but said nothing.

At Dax I had a card from Germaine. It had a happy tone and I hoped her depression was easing a bit:

"Hoping Italian riding a bicycle uphill goes well. Fed up with Stromboli. Might even join you. Reading a great book called *Forty Years with the Gas, Light & Coke Company*. Can't put it down. Sorry I called you a secondhand car dealer. Miss you, Germaine."

I scribbled a note back and hoped she was still at the Stromboli.

"Dear Diva, Uphill Italian going well. Reading a stunner myself—*How to Push a Pig in a Wheelbarrow Around France*. Car dealer? Have a nice Chevvy pickup, one lady owner, low mileage, make an offer. Do come if you can, Love, T."

* * *

Mountains at last. Pau to Luchon. Now things would change. Sprinters and time trialists would be put in their place.

Along with Romain, there were two fancied and dangerous climbers—our own Barbossa and the Spaniard Langarcia. My money was on Romain, although you couldn't dismiss the other two. And Vito? The wild card.

The field kept together until the gradients began to bite, then the thinning out began. The overcast sky and high wind promised a grim slog ahead. I'd managed to get the use of a small 4x4 and left Boretti to look after the main team. Getting myself classed a 'second team vehicle' wasn't easy.

After about an hour the weather worsened and riders paused to put on their transparent jackets as the rain came on with increasing velocity, easing as the race crossed the 2,114 meter Tourmalet and the 1,480 meter Col d'Aspin. Together Romain, Langarcia and Barbossa topped the Col de Peyresoudre where they faced a nightmarish descent through a heavy downpour that had come on like there was no tomorrow.

Behind, the field spread out for fear of being involved in some nasty crash, but at the same time they couldn't spread too far. I'd seen it done many times. A more daring rider could simply freewheel away from his rivals. So bad were the sudden conditions that the same thought must have dogged the three climbers, the realization that perhaps they should stay together and live to fight it out in less hazardous circumstances.

I was there, of course, in case Barbossa and Romain got into trouble. One, two, three—rain soaked they hurtled downward.

Suddenly, without any team support and for no advantage that I could see, Langarcia went for a flyer. Romain and Barbossa, clutching at brakes that were too wet to work and with eyes glazed from concentration, fought to keep the Spaniard in sight through the driving horizontal rain.

I kept the little Suzuki as close as possible to Barbossa although there were moments when the screen wipers barely coped. I had the hood up but with the sides open the mechanic and myself were almost as wet as the riders. If I'd had an umbrella I could have done a Gene Kelly.

The bend was almost a blind curve to the right: only by standing on the brakes did I miss ploughing into Barbossa sprawled in the road. The Suzuki aquaplaned, slewing broadside on, just missing the immobile Barbossa but flattening his machine. Behind me I could hear the screech of brakes as following vehicles skidded to a stop.

Barbossa was my problem, not so Romain and Langarcia, who both kept going, taking the advantage that was suddenly theirs.

Good old Boretti. Foreseeing possible accidents, he was close behind with a first-aid medic. Together we got Barbossa into the larger vehicle, turning it with great difficulty to meet up with the rapidly approaching ambulance that Boretti had radioed for. My quick impression of Barbossa's injuries was of bad cuts, bruises, and a concussion. Whether less or more serious, he was out of the race.

After about twenty minutes I caught up with Romain and Langarcia. The image of Barbossa's crash was foremost in every rider's mind, acting on their reflexes like a brake.

I saw Romain drop behind Langarcia long enough for the Spaniard to miss seeing him flick a gear change and then come past. Inside thirty seconds Romain had gained a short lead. He flung his machine into curve after curve, his frozen soaking face riveted on the road for any ruts which could put him in the same ambulance next to Barbossa.

Romain's attack had come near the end of the descent. Soon he was on a slightly more level stretch on a road he knew quite well. Somewhere beyond the greyness was Luchon.

How I hated that sort of weather and the memories it carried. It had thrown the whole race into confusion with the conditions slowing the motor cavalcade as much as it had hit the riders.

Normally Romain would have known where his team was, how far away they were, and how his rivals were placed. Yet there he was, and I knew how he must have felt, riding in an isolated world where all he could do was bash on, silently praying he wouldn't puncture or crash.

Then I had to hang back, well behind Romain's and Langarcia's rapidly closing team vehicles. In theory I had no business there, but I had two reasons why I was. Romain had long been a friend, despite the bit of bother over his fiancée—and besides, I wanted very much to keep him in the race. Without him anything spectacular Vito did would seem less of an achievement.

But onward and downward Romain continued his dangerous drop to put as much space between Langarcia and himself. When I looked in the mirror, I could just make out the Spaniard still coming on, drawing nearer I thought, although I couldn't be certain. And way back beyond Langarcia other riders were coming into view. Nothing for it but to keep driving and stay as close as I could legally get to Romain.

As the swine of a road rushed up to meet him, I could see he was sweeping corners as wide as possible so that the machine wasn't angled too sharply, the wet and the cold likely blurring his attention. At one point I came quite near and saw the slosh hosing from his wheels strike the screen like shotgun pellets. I knew well enough the battle he was fighting between caution and chance, trying not to think what could happen if luck went against him.

Eventually, glowing thoughts on crossing the finishing line must have filled his head. The rain eased slightly for a moment and spectators began rising magically out of the ground. There were no shortcuts, no team, just those cold numb legs to keep turning.

Was it the effects of long concentration, or simply the thought of a hot bath and dry clothes? He would keep looking 'round trying to spot Langarcia.

I heard my mechanic's voice follow mine as we both shouted "Oh, no!" Down Romain went, sliding sideways across the road, his feet still held to the pedals and the bike somersaulting with him. Boretti was at his side seconds after Romain had slid to a standstill. Quickly Boretti untangled him from the twisted cycle. Beyond Romain and Boretti, I glimpsed spectators and officials moving like ghosts in all directions, oblivious to the ceaseless downpour. And through that downpour I caught the hunched grey image of Langarcia as he sped past.

"Listen," I hissed over Boretti's shoulder above the racket. "Looks like you're badly grazed and pretty shaken. I might be wrong. If the medics give you the green light, somehow get back on. You're nearly home, nearly there. Look, some of your team's caught us up. They're here, waiting. Even if you can't ride they can push you..."

Boretti moved to one side. "Terry's right. Langarcia will take the stage, but you're up on him anyway."

We stood back while a couple in white coats, themselves soaked to the skin, gave him a fairly good workover before bandages and plasters came out. Their efforts were protected by the umbrella of a spectator held over them. A team mate was already waiting with a fresh machine.

"I can't ride, can't ride," he kept saying while Boretti echoed "You can, you can, don't give up now."

I leaned 'round Boretti's heavy carcass and seized Romain's arm. "Just get to the finish. You can still win the Tour de France. Things will be easier tomorrow."

I turned to his waiting team riders: there were four of them. "I don't care if you die on the way, but get him there. You'll have to push and you'll have to pull. Don't fail him now. He's still got a chance. Go on!"

It wasn't possible the four could all work at once; only two at a time could push or pull. First the giant Belgian Eddie de Beauplan and his slimmer brother Roger almost frogmarched Romain to a waiting cycle and eased him on to it.

They moved achingly slow at first, cursing the rain, cursing the Tour, cursing everyone. Romain's jerky legs began to turn as the Belgians dragged him along. The other two team riders rode ahead, then dropped back to do their stint at keeping the ailing Romain in motion.

I followed Boretti's vehicle and had to watch helplessly the slow painful progress. The de Beauplan brothers, gasping, mouths drooling, sweat mingling with rain, almost ground to a standstill until the other two took over and the Belgians rested, freewheeling, wiping their faces with towels Boretti had handed them.

Stupidly, all I could do was shout, "Push, Roger, push. You'll make it. Hang on. The road'll level out soon. Keep pedaling, Romain. Just get there. Tomorrow's another day."

Maybe, maybe not, perhaps my words had some effect. Gradually his rhythm picked up and the pushes eased. Looking far from being a winner, he freewheeled over the finishing line and disappeared among a mass of reporters.

I didn't see him till much later, having first seen to Vito, who'd plodded cautiously on, alone but not last. We met up in our allocated bedroom.

"Can Romain still win? Personally I doubt it." Despite Vito's immaculate appearance and scrubbed features, they didn't belie the tired man inside that tailored track suit.

"Not looking good," I admitted. "He's back to eleventh place, twelve minutes down, not on Langarcia who's third, but on van Faigneart who, like you, kept plodding. King of the Mountains? He'll get that all right simply on points.

The Izoard? By then he should have fully recovered. More to the point, how do you feel? That was a shocker out there today, both Barbossa and Romain going down."

"Me? Oh, fine," he sighed, slumping into a nearby chair and smiling at the obvious contradiction.

Although relatively flat between the Pyrénées and the Alps, there were enough minor climbs for a bandaged Romain to pick up more points. The exception came when the race moved inland to take in the famous climb up Mont Ventoux, the fourteen-mile Giant of Provence. Romain, now mostly recovered, took it in great form. And he did it in brilliant sunshine that seemed to add something to a memorable day, made even better by the appearance of Rosie and Margaret. Rosie and I exchanged quiet grins when Margaret flung her arms around Romain.

"Ain't love grand," I murmured.

"It's not restricted to young ones," Rosie said with a gentle nudge in my ribs.

"Oh, you're right. But we'd better keep our distance until you've sorted out your life." I don't know why I said this. Perhaps Germaine had something to do with it.

She kicked one of her sandals off and drew a pattern in the soil with her big toe. "Yes," she said quietly. "Too many dramas at once isn't a good idea. And I know the next few days are important to you. You've told me a bit about Vito, but really, why is his ride so important?"

I put my arm around her. The sun had lost some of its edge. The warmth of Rosie's body added to the sun felt good and comforting.

"Vito's ride is only important, mostly, to Corkscrew. Secretly I believe it's very important also to Vito himself. And to me somewhat. Beyond all that, there's no importance at all. As Germaine will insist on calling it—an old Italian riding a bike uphill."

"You like her, don't you, this Germaine?"

Unconsciously at first, I realized I'd taken my arm away from Rosie.

"Sure, she's an interesting person. But really we're worlds apart. Like with many people you touch then ricochet away."

She took my arm and put it back 'round her waist. "And Vito?"

"A complex, proud man, hard to know, yet I respect and like him. Although he's never won much, he really belongs to a blood line of campionissimi stretching from Girardengo through Guerra, Binda, Bartali, and Coppi. That's hard for you to understand, I know. You see, Bartali once as a young twenty-four year old, and later at thirty-four and thirty-five, rode away on his own from the Tour de France such was his power on the Col d'Izoard. He towed Coppi in 1949, otherwise there wasn't another rider in sight. This is what Vito hopes to do, to recapture what was once the golden age. Madness? Foolish pride? Probably. Middle-aged men playing silly games."

She squeezed my hand and kissed the side of my face. "No it's not. It's important to you, so it is important. We'd better go and prise Margaret and Romain apart. Come on."

* * *

Thankfully, there was a rest day at Carpentras. Both Vito and Romain opted for a quiet relaxing time. With the big battles ahead, there wasn't much to say: both had been through it all many times, chewing it over, the ifs and buts.

So I followed their example and found a reasonably quiet corner in an unpopular café. Around midday, Boretti came in holding papers and letters.

"There you are, Terry. A letter forwarded from Paris. You're lucky it's found you."

I saw straightaway that it was from Germaine. Inside a single sheet of Stromboli notepaper.

Dear Terry,

I hate goodbyes, particularly to you, so call me a coward if you like. I've spoken to Paul, my husband, on the phone several times and have decided, with conditions, to go back to him. A loveless but secure life almost as dull as my current reading—*The Decline of the Spoon-Making Industry in Samoa, 1907–1911.*

I'll always treasure the moments we spent together, even though we never got very close in the accepted sense of the word. A secondhand car salesman? No, an English gentleman. As sure as the turning of the Earth, you will always be someone special, and I'll never forget you.

Please stay in touch from time to time. My address is on the back. And my real name is Louise Lorrimare, but think of me always as Germaine.

I hope your Italian riding uphill works out for you both. Who knows? You might make it to California someday.

It was sort of love, wasn't it?

Germaine

The rest of the day passed unnoticed, as I relived my times with her. In total they weren't much, nor were they very close. Just talks with a woman I fancied, a woman I knew very little about. An English gentleman! That's a laugh.

I had a few moments when I felt like dashing off a letter to her with a plea to come back. But back to what? I hadn't the sort of money she was used to, barely enough to see me out in a not over-flush lifestyle. I guess we didn't have much in common. And yet...

And yet there was Rosie, dear Rosie, more my type of person.

The pressure of Vito's looming ride pushed Germaine from my thoughts for the time being.

20. Today a Rooster, Tomorrow a Feather Duster

Gap to Briançon: the famous stage, fought over by men forgotten, men remembered. Although the forecast was okay, that evening heavy black clouds waltzed in, and by eleven o'clock that night the sky gave a firework display.

Every square meter of accommodation was chock-full of cyclists, team people, journalists, TV crews, officials. Parked caravans, tents, and vehicles that housed unlucky spectators who'd missed out.

The race leaders were getting the full treatment. Earlier, flash bulbs had joined with the zig-zag lightning to create a hellzapoppin atmosphere. At last the place quietened down. I was with Vito again sharing a small twin-bed backroom in one of the pensions.

Toward midnight it began to hail. He'd been lying on his bed, still and silent, me keeping very quiet and willing him to fall asleep. Then he suddenly got up and sat by the small window. He was sideways on to me, the lightning showing his silhouette in stark flashes. I thought he looked like a statue, a cardboard cut-out, his Roman nose seeming out of proportion to the rest of his head.

"Can't you sleep?"

After a long pause he replied, "No."

"It would be a damn good idea if you could." In those noisy conditions I couldn't be sure, but for a few brief seconds I thought maybe he was crying.

Then he came back to his bed and flopped gently on it, like perhaps he was in pain. Putting on my best cheery voice, I said stupidly, "Well, this is it. The big day at last."

I had to strain to hear his words. "It all started out as a sort of joke, didn't it?"

I pushed myself into a sitting position.

"A sort of joke, sure. Somehow along the way it's got more, hasn't it?"

"Yes," he said, sighing. "A lot more. At first it was important to Corkscrew, and I went along with that. To him it was something mythical, something there are no words for. I think that's rubbed off onto me."

A flash of lightning lit the room. He was looking at me. "I think you feel that now, too, don't you?"

It hadn't really hit me that hard until then because I'd been tied up with the day to day happenings. But yes, he

181

was right. Perhaps not mythical, but maybe strangely important. No, not really important but final—the end of something, a thing that had to be done, proven, like Corkscrew had said. So I replied, "It's kind of winding things up, isn't it? For all of us.

"Whatever happens, you'll quit tomorrow for sure. The last kilometers you'll ever ride. Funny, but all this is just between you and me and Corkscrew, and no-one else knows much about it, not properly. You could have won the Tour several times if you'd really wanted, been up there with the immortals, instead..."

"Instead?" Through the gloom I could still see he was looking at me. "Instead? I remember you used to be fond of quoting those words of Brando's—'I coulda been somebody, I coulda been a contender'."

I had a spurt of memory, incidents from races long forgotten, mostly ones I didn't win. "Fancy you remembering that. Even if you pull it off tomorrow it'll soon be yesterday's news."

"Your lady film star thinks it's all a bit pitiful, doesn't she?"

Vito had sensed that all right. You can be fond of a woman and have a lot in common, but usually there's some bloody thing or other that divides you. Cycle racing strikes her as odd, a non-event, silly even. It's on the cards that if I was hitched to her she might want to see me wearing two-tone winklepickers and a Frank Sinatra hat and go mixing it with the mega-Frankensteins. "Yes, Germaine and I had quite a conversation about it, but I kept it short. How can you explain to people like her? It brings Corkscrew's funny old world to mind."

Thoughtfully he said, "Poor old Corkscrew. I'd like to win for him. Being as sick as he is, I wonder if he'll make it long enough to witness it, win or lose."

"We can't do more. There's a huge TV at his bedside. For our futures—what? You're okay, you've got all those Silvanas and Juliettes to go back to, back to the family estates and all that wine. Me, I'm not sure what I want."

"You don't sound too happy about it," he ventured. "In your heart I suppose you're like the majority of people—you want comfortable wealth, the ideal partner, and freedom. True, the future doesn't look too bright. We somehow have to find a niche and let the robber barons get on with it. Just as long as they don't think we don't know."

While he was speaking, an anecdote I'd read came into my mind. He sensed I was quietly laughing to myself. "What is it?" he said.

"Huh. It's just something I read somewhere. There was this patient in hospital. The doc had one of those internal scanners up the bloke's bum. The patient asked the doc what he could see. 'The future,' came the reply."

We sat grinning to ourselves. With Vito it soon passed. The tension coming off him was electric, so much so that I racked my mind for something light to say. "Here," I said as I dredged the mind. "Don't know if I ever told you, or told anyone, but when I was a 'cycling youth' of about seventeen, I had this daydream, this fantasy, where I was within a couple of minutes of winning an imagined Tour of Britain. Ahead of me were a couple of the world's best pros. I couldn't overhaul them.

This girl I was in love with arranged an accompanying jeep to cruise behind me with a gramophone playing Chopin's Polonaise. As a youngster I found it 'inspiring'. Silly sods at that age, weren't we?"

I don't think my story amused him or even if he'd actually heard it. "And of course I won," I added.

"Yes," came a vague reply which could have been an answer to anything.

Neither spoke for about half an hour. It was well past midnight. He went over to the window again. By then the storm had moved away, although distant lightning still sent quick flashes across the room.

"Bit different in Bartali's day," I muttered cautiously in case he wanted to pretend he hadn't heard. But he moved and it seemed my words brought him back to his bed.

"I was thinking the same thing," he said. "He had to have earplugs because fans stood outside where he was sleeping, calling his name. No-one's calling mine. They're all asleep."

"Does it scare you a bit? Tomorrow, I mean."

"What's the time?" he asked.

"The time? Why? Middle of the bloody night."

"Napoleon said that true courage is the courage of two a.m."

21. You Dropped the Tour

I was tied up with last minute details and having to edge my way through the crowds. I turned quickly when someone grabbed my arm.

"You're still at it, then?"

It was Georgina Winters.

"Christ, what are you doing here? Come to see the king of the mountains do his stuff?"

She had on a large straw hat that rested on her eyebrows. "Sort of. Why not?"

"I Suppose you wish you'd stayed with that ad project?"

She used the finger of one hand to push the hat's brim up on to her forehead. "You can't win them all. I see he's well on course."

I couldn't resist it. "You two had a bit of a fling, didn't you?"

She smiled and studied the back of her hand before giving me a gentle shove and turning back into the crowd. "He reminded me of a boy I knew when I was younger." The straw hat disappeared among the pressing throng.

After I'd helped Boretti get the team in order and checked everything, I went looking for Vito and found him surrounded by journalists. I edged my way through the crowd and immediately saw what had caused this sudden interest. Vito wasn't wearing the team jersey which carried the advertisers' names and turned him into a pedaling ad. Instead he had on the Italian national green-red-white jersey, as worn in the old days. Across the chest was the single word Bartali. I waited till the photographers had done their work and the small crowd found interest elsewhere. I took his arm and led him into a nearby corner. He stood there with his hands on his hips, a faint smile gradually spreading.

"Are you going to tell me about it?" I asked, sucking my teeth.

He sat down on one of the folding chairs. "What is there to tell? I hope it brings me luck. I've had it for years. It was one of his team's jerseys and has never been worn."

"Until now. I doubt they'll let you start. Boretti will go mad."

"I'll chance it. What can they do? These are my last hours as a professional cyclist whatever happens out there today."

"Well, I said, dragging up a chair, "keep out of sight until the last moment. I doubt they'll hold up the start because of a jersey. Probably some sort of fine will come into it."

He waved my words aside. "The last hours, Terry. The clock's ticking. You've ridden your last—how does it feel?"

We'd both skirted around talking about this. Perhaps Vito had saved it till the last minute.

"There aren't words to describe it," I said quietly. "Perhaps it's a mix of sadness, relief, fear, bewilderment, emptiness."

"I can understand that," he said, nodding. "I think that's how I'll feel. In a way it's like dying and being reborn."

I'll never forget the look on Boretti's face when he clapped eyes on Vito. He actually walked around him a couple of times without speaking, as if he'd seen a ghost.

I got in first. "It'll be okay. Just a little good luck quirk of his. Don't forget this is his swan-song. Best you know it now. Corkscrew's money went into this moment."

For a second I thought Boretti was going to punch me. Instead he shook his head and threw up his arms in despair. "Now you tell me," he said and went back to his waiting team.

Luckily it ended on a light moment. As Vito went to take up his place in the team line up, an elderly Italian grabbed his arm. "Maestro! Campionissimo!" he cried.

Obviously a man with a memory that stretched back to when Vito's jersey meant something. Even Boretti managed a stiff smile.

The peloton stayed together climbing the Col de Vars. No-one was going to break with the Izoard coming next. Romain collected more points when he made a dash at the summit.

On the descent the field strung out, loosely regrouping at the bottom. Everyone knew it was here on the 2,630 meter Izoard that Romain would make his big move. He was quite aware that Vito was going to attempt his break, yet I'm sure Romain firmly believed the Italian was past it, a ghost from another age, there because of misplaced vanity. The four riders who had latched on to Romain were of more concern, among them the Spanish climber Langarcia.

As the gradient steepened and the miles of climbing began, one by one the followers fell back. All except Vito.

There was a touch of contempt in Romain's backward glance. He even smiled, thinking he now had the Izoard to himself.

Wanting to stay as close as possible, I'd switched to a pillion ride on one of the Tour's motorcycles.

As the four dropped riders fell further back, a man pushed himself forward into the path of Romain and Vito, shouting in Italian—"Go, great Vito, They'll never catch you now." Words that tumbled around in my brain.

I saw Vito's head turn and caught his smile as he lifted a hand.

Of course Romain hadn't really started yet and was edging his way through a tunnel of spectators followed by a stoic Vito close behind. A strange silence had descended on the mass of spectators, like a communal holding of the breath. And yet already a strange two-man duel had begun to take shape with an increasingly strong head wind adding a further obstacle. National flags and placards of encouragement began to snap and tug as the wind's ferocity increased.

In front of me was Romain's team vehicle, mechanics ready with spare wheels and a couple of extra cycles. They were grinning at me for my closeness to Vito. In their eyes Vito counted for nothing. It was the highly placed Frenchman Audaire and Van Faigneart behind who were the real threat, both having time in hand, fast and dangerous once away from the mountains. Our main vehicle, for what it was worth that day, kept close to Vito's team back down the Col.

Tight faced Tour officials ogled the scene from their Landrover, probably irked that the lowly placed Vito had tagged along to detract from Romain's big solo effort to win the Tour. Ahead of them came another vehicle housing the TV camera crews and radio commentators.

For a moment I had the terrible impression that Vito was beginning to fade already. No, it had been a surge by Romain stretching the gap further. Vito's eyes flashed,

189

but he didn't panic, didn't alter his pace, still playing it like I knew he would. I couldn't help noticing the sinews on his slim brown arms looked tight enough to burst.

Romain threw a couple of rapid glances behind, wondering why Vito wasn't meters away. Instead, and without it hardly showing, Vito had drawn nearer. A flash of disbelief crossed Romain's face. He stood on his pedals, out of the saddle, gripping his bars tighter and tighter.

Just then Romain's team car edged past to have a few words with him. I saw him shrug and smile as he looked around at the Italian as if to say—Who cares? If you could ever finish ahead of me you're so far down on time. What does it matter if you're tagging along?

And still that uncanny silence. I couldn't make it out. There was the odd cry, the calling of a name. I'd thought we'd be deafened by the shouting. Yes, sure, there were bursts of muttering and some hand clapping. Certainly it wasn't lack of interest, because I could still detect a sort of intense low hum of emotion.

The picture changed again as the gradient swung a little to the right. Romain had definitely carved himself more space. By then there must have been fifteen meters separating them. Again Romain's head turned as he tried to tell from Vito's granite-like features how much fight there was still in him. He knew full well he could ignore, forget, the Italian. Still, I knew Romain. Pride, that's what it was. You couldn't tell a thing from Vito's face: I certainly couldn't, and neither could Romain. For Vito was riding like an automaton, always with that look as if his mind was far away drawing inspiration from something, somewhere, only he knew.

I snatched a quick look at Romain. His jaw moved as if he were grinding his teeth. He was all motion, side to side, up, down, yet not without a certain style. Behind him the man almost old enough to be his father, imperturbable, fixed, coming on, coming on…

Mile after mile the slow struggle continued. This wasn't speeding racing cyclists that flash across the nightly TV screens. It reminded me of a dream in slow motion, slow enough for cheeky spectators to jog next to the riders, neither rider even noticing them. Both were far away in another world, fighting the gale, the dust, heat and gradient, fighting each other. For Romain there was only Vito, for Vito only Romain. Nothing and nobody counted as the endless slog ground on.

When I turned to look back down the Col, winding away as far as I could see, there wasn't another rider in sight. If nothing else, Vito had done his Bartali. He'd dropped the Tour de France.

Then Romain began trying an old trick he was fond of. He'd slow just a bit so that the gap shrunk. As Vito automatically came closer, Romain switched from side to side achieving nothing except startling a few close spectators. Vito? He didn't seem to notice, didn't alter his pace, his position, anything, as if to say—Okay Romain, play at silly buggers.

It comes back to me how I felt then, how both men were my friends and how I wanted the best for both of them. I was overawed by Vito's riding and glad that Romain would be pulling back much of his lost time.

As Romain turned his head more often, you could still see the annoyance on his face, annoyance that this old Italian who should have retired years ago could still challenge him. But there was a long way yet to Briançon. Romain must have been thinking the whole time that Vito couldn't last, that soon he'd crack.

In better circumstances I'd have smiled at Vito's little foibles. He'd pulled a small pad—cologne soaked, I'm sure— from the pocket in his jersey and wiped it across his face. Quickly he threw it away and a grinning souvenir hunter grabbed it.

At last there was a sudden rising roar, slow at first, then building fast. The crowds had come to life shedding their hypnotic daze. Vito had attacked! He'd drawn level with Romain. Side by side they slogged it out. I was being driven as close as I could possibly get. Vito sensed I was there and half turned. As he did so, sweat and spittle flew. Blood too. I guess he'd bitten his lip or tongue.

"You've dropped the Tour!" I yelled. Did my words strike home? Our eyes met in a glance, mine staring and anxious, his mere slits through the dusty sweat plastered on his face.

I couldn't shed the sadness I felt as space opened up once more and Romain pulled further away to something about a twenty meter gap. Romain's face like that of any young super-fit pro showed little suffering, just a mix of tension, effort, annoyance and sweat. In contrast, Vito's whole countenance was beginning to register something I didn't like. Great suffering? Well, certainly. God knows what his body was going through, or his legs which must have felt like lead.

Thirty meters of space. It looked like Vito had lost the act. What could you say of a man his age (and mine) whose legs had metaphorically, or literally, ridden 'round the world a few times.

Yet one could only admire him. His position hadn't changed. Still he sat there in the middle of the road, still upright, those old legs turning out the power. And you know what? That gap had narrowed. Down to about twenty meters, maybe fifteen and closing.

We were still driving as near as we could get. What I saw was incredible. Vito's eyes were actually closed yet he held that centre road position as if he were on rails.

If he could have heard me above the shouting, I'd have called Stop! Call it a day! He'd not been disgraced. He'd done what the rest of the race couldn't match. To even stay in sight of Romain on a mountain was triumph enough.

Romain was aware he was still being closely tailed and was out of the saddle again, piling on all the pressure he could find, certain as I was that Vito was close to folding up. Somehow, though, it all had a touch of the miraculous. In all my years as a pro, I'd seen nothing quite like it. I've watched men fade, explode, get off their bike and hurl it away and crawl into the sag wagon. As I've done myself! Unbelievably the space between them had shrunk yet again. Yes, it had actually narrowed. And yes! Vito was almost on to Romain's wheel! Nor did he stop. Again they were side by side, punching it out, a battle of the giants. Vito's face was now a mask, screwed up so I hardly recognised the man I'd known for years. Veins standing out as if to burst, hands like claws, eyes half closed. I don't think Romain could believe it. He too was gasping as maximum effort poured out of him. At that moment I could read his thoughts—Crack, sod you, crack!

How I hoped the cameras had caught it all and that Corkscrew had seen it. I still can't find words to do justice to what was happening that day among the wisping clouds hugging the Izoard. As if to add to the drama, an eagle or big hawk appeared overhead and, even that too seemed riveted on what was happening below.

Disbelief!—then it was Romain on Vito's wheel! Romain, out of the saddle still, throwing his body weight onto his tiring legs. I couldn't believe this. Vito had dropped him, dropped the king of the mountains, and was pulling away.

Then it was Romain's turn to stop that widening space, those dreadful meters that meant everything. I really didn't know what Vito was trying to prove. He'd done what he set out to do, ridden in the ghostly wheel-tracks of Bartali and Coppi and left the Tour far behind. No-one would have blamed him if he'd got off then and called it a day. Win or lose there on the big Col, what Vito had done should go down in the annals of the Tour de France. Sure, he'd had to get into the lead somehow or the knockers would have said that Romain towed him. Questions peppered my brain. Could he last out? Could he hold on till Briançon? Or would Romain have found that extra punch to go past him, as I've seen him do many times against other riders? Right then it was anybody's guess.

I wish I'd never seen what happened next, but the TV cameras had caught it anyway. I assumed Vito had used a little coloring to hide the greying on his temples, and massive sweating had caused the coloring to run down the sides of his face.

Real trouble, though, was building up for him. I wasn't alone in seeing that. His legs seemed to be turning in jerky stabs. All rhythm had gone out of them. His eyes were open, eyes that appeared to see nothing. They were the glassy eyes of a dead man staring through a grimy mask.

As for Romain, he was some twenty paces behind, hard pressed, giving all he'd got yet unable to close. I was sure something awful was happening to Vito. Probably no-one else had noticed it, but I've been there before. We accelerated through ahead of the race.

It was bad. It had to stop, it had to end. Right then.

But I couldn't stop anything. No-one was listening. Vito was ahead of Romain but in trouble. I mean, real trouble. I called out "Vito, Stop!" Get off! You've won, you've done it!" I caught my breath and nearly choked.

A voice—it was mine—said "Dear God, he's fallen." Vito hit the road, wheels spinning, dust rising.

It's a blank now, but somehow I found myself next to him. I know I was holding his head and motorcycle escorts were keeping the pressing crowd at bay. I remember too glancing up in time to see Romain plug slowly past, looking back, wondering.

"Vito, the ambulance is coming, hold on." He was the color of chalk. I hadn't a clue what was wrong. Was this how things end? Him? Me? In the dust on some bloody mountain with everybody staring? After all the years, the miles, in some ditch. Dear God, it wasn't right, wasn't right…

* * *

Two Years Later

Two years, two more Tours de France that Romain didn't win. Time hasn't dimmed that image which comes now in the slow motion of memory of Vito going down, dust rising, like a stricken bull elephant shot by hunters. Crystal clear still is the sound of the rising helicopter taking him to the hospital at Cannes. He survived the heart attack: thankfully he's a tough old bird. There had been a weakness no-one had suspected.

I see him when I can, but there isn't a lot to say. Much of his flamboyance has gone. He even drives a modern car. I wondered if his warrior was sleeping or still alive inside his silence. For over a year he never mentioned the Izoard, and neither did I. Then, about six months ago while we were talking, he suddenly said quietly, "I did it, didn't I?" I took his outstretched hand and shook it. All I said was "Campionissimo." We've never mentioned it since. What I thought would be a Tour landmark, a legend, appears to be forgotten history. Perhaps Germaine was right—he was simply an old Italian riding a bike uphill. So much for glory, magic, and heroism.

The lovely cuddly Rosie is with me now. Love? I remember reading once that at our level of being we don't really know what it means, and all we have are degrees of affection. Like Paula, she's too good for me. Sometimes Paula's memory haunts me. If I had my time again, I'd treat her very differently. The only time we disagreed in all those years was when I wore my cycle trouser clips in bed to stop my pyjama legs riding up.

Sure, I suppose I still fancy Germaine, and I get a strong sense of her when she drops me a line—even though the letters are full of bizarre book titles. She says she's not particularly unhappy, whatever that means.

Corkscrew left me his money, turning that year between my two Tours as one of rags to riches. I've given a lot to Throbbo to expand his café into a swish restaurant proper. On an empty site nearby we plan to build a cycle centre and museum. With Corkscrew's money came his cycle collection, among which, well spread about, were his guns. In anticipation, he'd earlier packed the stuff himself.

I spend a lot of time looking up old riders, collecting their stories and any memorabilia that's going. And I still manage a couple of hours on the bike most weeks. I let go Corkscrew's ashes on the Izoard. It was mid winter, cold and dark, but with my eyes closed I swear that on the wind came the roar and hubbub of the passing Tour de France. Ghosts were everywhere.

Romain and Margaret are to marry once this year's Tour ends. I've bought them a family hotel in Provence for their future.

Of the three Izoard participants, I'm the only one left who sees it as something like we'd originally envisaged. Corkscrew has gone, and I think Vito must bitterly regret it. Perhaps after all, it wasn't the end of things. For me, anyway, that year of my last Tour was a new beginning.

Funny old world, innit?

About the Author

Ralph Hurne burst on the literary scene in 1973, when his cycle racing novel *The Yellow Jersey* quickly became a runaway success. It has been hailed as "sports fiction at its best" by *The New York TImes Book Review,* and "the greatest cycling novel ever written" by *Bicycling Magazine*, and the book has been translated into a dozen other languages.

Born and raised in England, but now retired and living in Australia, Hurne has been employed in just about every aspect of literary work, from librarian to copy-writer and from feature writer to editor.

A cyclist almost before he could walk, bicycles have always featured large in his life. As a member of the long defunct British League of Racing Cyclists, his most active years were when the BLRS finally embraced continental style open-road racing in Britain.

Publisher's Weekly calls his writing "full of charm, excitement and intelligence, and *The New York Times Book Review* stated that he has "a cool, downbeat style descended from Lardner and Hemingway, and a fine hand with the hairpin turns of suspense."